WICKED LOVE

SAVAGELY DEPRAVED

J.L. QUICK

COPYRIGHT

Cover Design: Morally Gray Publishing
Editing: Spice Me Up Editing (Katie)
Proofreading: Spice Me Up Editing (Kendra)

To the wicked ones that enjoy their hand necklaces good and tight...

You might want to hold your breath.

AUTHOR'S NOTE

This novel is a contemporary dark romance. It contains scenes and descriptive adult content, recommended for adult (18+) readers.

As a contemporary dark romance, this novel is not intended to be a portrayal of a healthy relationship or a 'how to guide' for the kink and lifestyle elements depicted within.

For those interested in exploring aspects of kink and/or dominant-submissive relationships explored in the following chapters, please do so responsibly and with appropriate reference materials.

TRIGGER WARNINGS

This novel is a contemporary dark romance. It contains scenes and descriptive adult content that might be triggering for some readers.

Please review the content warnings at the link below.

THE DEVILS OF ADELAIDE COVE

"I love you with so much of my heart that none is left to protest."

— **William Shakespeare, Much Ado About Nothing**

BEFORE YOU GET STARTED...

Wicked Love is the continuation of the Savagely Depraved series. To fully understand the events that are going to unfold in these pages, I highly recommend starting with Dark Devils, (the prequel novella to the Savagely Depraved series) and Family Ties.

Both are available for purchase on Amazon.

CHAPTER
ONE

SAMUEL

My hand trembles as I press the doorbell. I barely register the sound of it chiming inside the house, my eyes are entirely fixated on my shaking hand. Lifting the other, I stare at them both while I wait for someone to answer the door.

Cuts.

Scratches.

Stained red and smelling of copper.

Dripping with blood.

The thick crimson liquid trails down my arms and over my hands. It trickles along of my fingers and drips from the tips, falling to the leather of my shoes and to the porch beneath my feet.

Pity, it's probably staining their beautiful porch.

Looking down, I catch sight of my shirt. Once white and pristine, it is now stained a deep shade of an intense ruby-red. The deep color of death continues to seep across the fabric covering my stomach and pools at my cufflinks with every pained breath that I take.

No answer.

Fuck!

Jesus, Grant. Pull your cock out of her and answer the fucking door.

Reaching out to press the button a second time, my jaw ticks at the realization that I left a bloody print with my first push.

Fuck!

Were there others?

Or was this the only one I left?

I press it again, holding it firmly until I hear it chiming throughout their home. As it begins to echo through the door, I pull back my finger. Untucking my shirt, I use an unsoiled spot to wipe my blood from their home.

I'll deal with the porch later.

If he doesn't kill me first.

"I'm coming," a sweet, feminine voice calls from the other side of the door, her voice growing louder with every syllable.

The door opens, and I'm met with Abigail's gorgeous face; her eyes immediately widen upon the sight of me. She swallows hard and takes a small step back, looking as though she desperately needs to put distance between the two of us.

The way my cock reacts to her presence, she is making a smart decision.

But tonight, the thought of sinking into her cunt is the last thing on my mind.

Well, it was.

Until I saw her.

"Aren't you going to invite me in?" I push out the words through the searing pain in my chest. Taking advantage of the small space she has left in the threshold, I nudge her out of the way as I help myself into their home.

"Grant!" Her voice trembles with fear as she calls for him.

It takes him only a second to react to the desperation in her voice, and he joins us in the foyer almost instantly. With how protective he is of her, I'm surprised he didn't come barreling into the hall to save her from me. He pauses briefly when he sees me—*I knew this was the last place I should have come*—and I can easily read the disdain on his face.

A blind man could fucking see it.

He wastes no time putting himself between me and Abigail. His movement is a very clear reminder that she is completely off-limits to me.

"I fucked up..." I mumble the words while stepping toward him and extending my bloodied hand before he has a chance to ask me the question we both know is on his mind.

Why did I come here?

CHAPTER
TWO

SAMUEL

About Two Months Ago

"Can I get a refill, beautiful?" I flag down the petite, young, brunette bartender to refill my beer.

She grabs a bottle from the under-bar fridge, pops off the cap, and places it in front of me. Leaning forward, she places her forearms on the bar and looks at me inquisitively before she says, "This doesn't seem like your kind of place."

She's not wrong.

The Rusty Anchor is a dive bar. From the outside, it looks condemned. The inside isn't much better, with burned-out lights and dust covering most surfaces. Nothing but bottled—*mostly warm*—beer. The floors are sticky. The barstools wobble. The clientele is questionable.

The warm beer and shitty atmosphere aren't why I'm here, though—*she is.*

"You look vaguely familiar, but I don't think I've seen you around here before," she presses with a raspy tone.

No, but I've seen you.

Four days ago, I ran into her walking down the street. It was likely inconsequential to her—just a little bump between strangers—but I haven't been able to stop thinking about her since.

The way her bright green eyes sparkled as she briefly glanced up at me. How fucking great those long, lean legs of hers would look wrapped around my waist as she took my cock. And I can't stop imagining what that raspy voice of hers will sound like when she's screaming as I take her.

Thoughts I know I won't be able to rid myself of until I get what I need—*to be buried inside of her as I completely overpower her petite body.*

"You haven't," I answer shortly. I'm not here to make small talk with her, but I'll do whatever is necessary to get her alone.

"You strike me more as the kind of guy that would visit The Rail." She continues to look me over. "The rich, stuffy assholes over there seem like much more your type."

"Did you just call me a rich, stuffy asshole?" I smirk before taking a sip of my room-temperature beer.

A slight blush of pink spreads over her cheeks as she quickly struggles to figure out how to respond. "I'm just saying. A guy like you. A place like this. If you were planning on slumming it, we don't exactly get a whole lot of single women in here."

"What about you?" I cock an eyebrow and her eyes widen slightly.

"What about me? Am I single?" she stammers slightly before breaking eye contact. "Yes."

Fuck, she's adorable.

"Do you think I'd be slumming it with you?" Her face drops slightly when I pause. "Because I think you're fucking stunning. Too fucking gorgeous and intriguing to be in a dump like this."

Her eyes fall to the floor, and my cock twitches as I watch the heated crimson creep up her neck and over her cheeks.

How have the men in this place not eaten this sweet girl alive yet?

Because I'm ready to have my fucking way with her right here on this bar top.

"Hey, Mia," a drunken, middle-aged man calls from the other end of the bar. "What the fuck do I have to do to get another beer around here?"

Looking up, she briefly makes eye contact with me before grabbing a beer and tending to the other waiting customers.

Mia...

As I nurse my beer, I flirt with her throughout the evening. While every man in this place can't keep their eyes off her, and they are quite vocal about it, I have something they don't.

Money.

A whole fucking lot of money.

The potential of a hefty tip alone will bring her back to me, but we both know that my interest in her is what keeps her standing in front of me. She is blinded by the possibilities of me—*so blinded that she doesn't see me for what I really am.*

I take the final swig from the bottle, and she is promptly here asking in a sultry tone, "Another? It's last call, and we're closing up in about ten minutes."

Placing a hundred dollar bill under my bottle, I slide it toward her side of the counter. "Two. And I'll split them with you once you lock up."

Her bright green eyes literally sparkle at my words as she pulls the cash and bottle from the bar. Tucking the money into her pocket, she nods, "Deal. I'll be out in about thirty minutes."

"Thirty minutes." I tip my head as I repeat it back to her before heading outside to my car.

CHAPTER
THREE

SAMUEL

While I sit in my car, I watch as the unseemly patrons continue to stumble out of the bar, counting the minutes on the dash display. My hand repeatedly palms over my throbbing cock, and I can't push the thought sinking inside of her from my mind.

Just a few minutes shy of her promised thirty minutes, she steps out of the doors. There are only two cars left in this parking lot—my shiny Maserati and what I am assuming is her rusted Chevy pickup.

She locks the doors to the bar and saunters cutely over to the back of the truck, dropping the tailgate and climbing onto it. Turning off the car, I leave my keys in the cupholder and climb out of the driver's seat.

Walking to the truck, I can't pull my eyes from the bare, crossed legs dangling from her perch. The short little denim skirt she's wearing barely covers her, inching higher as she shifts her weight like she's practically inviting me inside.

Patience, sweet girl.

As I get closer, she extends one of the beers toward me. Taking it from her, I take a sip and lightly shake my head. "I think we both know that I didn't actually stick around this dump for another warm beer."

Dipping her head, Mia tucks a loose tendril of hair behind her ear. I step closer, and I don't stop until her outer thigh is firmly resting against my hip. Still holding the bottle in my hand, I place my hands on the tailgate against each of her hips.

Without looking up, she meekly asks, "Then, what did you stay for?"

"You." My tone is soft yet firm. As the words resonate, she begins to lift her head. She looks up through her lashes, and her gaze meets mine; I'm surprised to find a glimmer of lust in her emerald eyes.

She might not be so sweet and innocent after all.

I take her lips the moment she lifts her face enough to make them accessible to me. They are soft and supple, and I want more of them. *I need more of them.* Swiping my tongue along the crease between them, she parts them for me. I plunge my tongue into her mouth and fervently begin my exploration of every part of her.

She meets my need, her fingers gripping the front of my shirt and fisting it tightly as she pulls me closer. Our tongues wrestle, fighting for control—*control I know she will never have.* Continuing to plunder her mouth, I grip her hips and begin to slide my hands down the bare skin of her thighs. Reaching her knees, I squeeze them firmly and start uncrossing them when she breathlessly pulls back from our kiss.

"Wait...," she pants, and her warm, beer-scented breath blows against my face, "I don't even know your name.

"Sam," I say against her lips.

"This is going really fast, Sam."

"Fuck, I love how my name sounds rolling off your tongue." I brush my lips over hers as I maneuver myself between her thighs. I slide her skirt up her thighs, needing to spread them wide enough for my broad frame, and leaving the bunched fabric resting around her waist. A light grumble rises from my chest as I stare down our bodies to the awaiting warmth between her thighs.

"Is it too fast?" I teasingly rub the backs of my knuckles over the skimpy, pink cotton thong covering her cunt. She whimpers slightly but otherwise stares back at me silently with her lusty eyes locked on mine. Slipping my finger under the cotton, I pull it to the side and am pleased to find her bare. Not breaking eye contact with her, I lower myself between her knees. "Is it too fast to want to taste you?"

She doesn't protest as I place a trail of wet, sloppy kisses up her inner thigh. Licking her pussy with a firm flick of my tongue, she lets out a soft groan.

And I'm done for.

Losing every bit of control, I grip her hips and drive my face into her cunt. I fervently lick and suck at her clit, needing nothing more than just hearing her scream my name. Rubbing a finger around her dripping entrance, I slip it inside of her teasingly slow.

Fuck, she's tight.

My cock is going to fucking ruin her.

Adding my thumb to the barrage of pleasure on her clit, I groan into her cunt as she begins to lose control. Her hips buck and rock against my face as I quickly work her toward the brink. She comes hard, filling the empty parking lot with her cries of pleasure.

"You taste so fucking good," I groan against her as I continue to lick at her sensitive clit. Her hands push at my face to ease the pressure, but I hold her thighs open with my forearms as I suck and lick even harder. Her trembling thighs fight against my hold, and my cock begins to grow painfully hard.

"The wetter you get, the sweeter you fucking taste," I tell her as I force her to come again. Standing between her knees, I gather her hands in one of mine and press them firmly to the bed of the truck. Holding her forcefully beneath me, I take her mouth and make her taste her delectable juices lingering on my tongue.

Pulling back from our kiss, I grab my beer and take a sip of it before placing it between her thighs. Her eyes widen as I rub the mouth of the bottle against her dripping cunt, and I can't help the smile on my face.

"I could drink from your sweet fucking cunt for days."

"Sam," she chuckles my name, not realizing the brevity of what's to come, "What are you doing?"

Sliding it into her, I grunt, "Whatever the fuck I want."

"Sam!" she gasps and struggles to pull out of my grip as I thrust the neck into her. "This isn't funny. Stop."

She continues to try and fight me as I fuck her cunt with the bottle.

She's even more stunning than before.

"Are you going to fill this bottle with your delicious fucking cum?" My question rhetorical as I listen to her uncontrollable moans of pleasure.

"Please. Sam. Stop," Mia cries as I relentlessly slide the smooth glass into her slick cunt.

CHAPTER
FOUR

SAMUEL

"Stop?" I taunt. "You don't mean that. I'm watching your tight little cunt squeeze around this bottle as you fight coming for me."

"Please..." A tear rolls down her face, and her body spasms when I drive the bottle deeper and force her to come yet again. Mercilessly, I continue to tease her with the neck, and she quivers around the brown glass sliding through her arousal.

"Are you going to come that hard around my cock?" I pull the bottle from her. I bring the glass up to my lips and lick her sweet arousal from it. I take a sip and groan as I swallow her down. Placing the bottle in the truck bed, I unzip my pants and pull out my cock, already dripping with precum.

"Sam!" she screams as I violently yank her toward me and sink the entirety of myself into her soaked cunt.

"Fuck," I moan, "it sounds even better than I imagined when you scream for me."

Continuing to hold her hands firmly against the cold metal of the truck, I wrap my free hand around her throat as I continue to drive into her to the hilt. I repeatedly slam every inch of me inside of her as she writhes and screams beneath me.

"You're so fucking tight when you scream," I grunt as I thrust into her. "It's even fucking better when you fight me."

Climbing on top of her, I release her hands, and they immediately begin to flail at me, trying to push me from inside of her. Outweighing her by easily one hundred pounds, her fight is futile. Yet it causes my cock to grow even more rigid inside of her.

"That's it," I groan with a smile, as her palm strikes across my face. "Fucking fight me. You can hate every second of it, but you won't be able to deny how much you fucking love me inside you when you're coming for me."

"Stop!" Her cries and screams continue to fill the void of the empty parking lot. Tears continue to stain her cheeks, and her tight cunt begins to tremble around my cock. Her eyes lock on mine as she tries unsuccessfully to shove me from her again before I can push her over the edge.

As much as she tries to fight it, she clenches uncontrollably hard as I tear her needed release from her. Violently thrusting through her tight vise, my balls tighten, and I know I can't hold back any longer. I let out a roar as I pull from her and paint my release on the ground beneath the tailgate.

I step back from the truck and tuck my spent cock back into my pants. Lifting the bottle I used to warm up Mia's perfect little cunt, I take another sip before pouring some into the pool of cum at my feet and kicking it into the dirt.

"You were better than I fucking dreamed." I grip her thigh as she tries to pull her skirt back down to cover herself. "If your needy cunt wants more—"

"Don't fucking touch me." She shoves my hand from her leg as she continues to sob.

"We both know you've never fucking come like that before," I chuckle, leaving her curled into a ball as I head to my car. "You can find me at The Rail if you change your mind."

Closing the door, I gun the engine and pull from the parking lot. Dust trails behind my car as my tires tear up the gravel and dirt. Taking another sip of my warm, cunty beer, I place it in the cupholder to enjoy the remainder at home.

At this hour, I make quick work of crossing through town, back to my side filled with sprawling estates and massive mansions.

Can't say I didn't invite her to join me...

Flipping on the blinker, I turn toward my drive and wait for the electronic sensor to open the gate before driving up to my home. I come to a stop at the base of the steps, leaving the car in the middle of the large circular drive. One of my staff will take care of it in the morning. Pushing open the door, I grab the beer bottle from the cupholder and head inside.

It's vacant. Too quiet. I need something to come home to at night.

I should probably get a dog.

But a woman would be so much more fun to play with.

If it's not going to be Mia, I need to find someone. Someone with a tight little cunt and a pretty mouth to stick my cock in when and where I please.

Sipping the beer as I walk through the house in the dark, I can't stop thinking about Mia. The way she thrashed beneath me and that look in her eyes when her body betrayed her, causing her to unwillingly lose herself around my cock.

Fuck, she would've been perfect.

Even my cock fucking agrees.

It's been less than thirty minutes since I was buried inside of her, and I'm already fucking hard again.

Walking into the living room, I place the bottle on an end table as I unzip my pants and pull out my cock. Taking a seat in an oversized, leather upholstered chair, I turn on the highlights I missed of tonight's game.

Beer in hand, I leisurely stroke my cock as I watch the recap. Then, once it's over, I click the remote to stream from an attached hard-drive of porn cultivated to my particular interests. Savoring the last of my Mia-flavored lager, my eyes glued to the screen before me, I fist my length until I spill over my hand.

DETECTIVE MICHALES

"Michales!" Chief yells through the office. "There's a woman out front who's looking to report an incident last night at the Rusty Anchor."

"Jesus Christ." I roll my eyes and sigh. "It's always that fucking shithole."

Pushing my chair back from my desk, I stand as I pull my gun from the top drawer of my desk. After I slip it into my holster, I round my desk to make my way to the front of the precinct.

"Michales," he huffs as he approaches. "It's a fucking rape allegation. Maybe find a bit of couth and sensitivity before you go fucking talk to her."

"Yes, Sir," I stammer, "Of course."

Without moving from my side, he eyes the office, and I'm all but certain he's looking for anyone else to send in my place. It's just me and Brown—a rookie who's only days out of the academy—leaving him no other option beside doing it himself.

"Don't make me regret this." He drops a slip of paper on my desk and turns on his heel to head back to his office.

I might be the office fuck up, but I'm apparently still good enough when no one else is around.

I lift the paper and read the name scribbled across it.

Mia Dillon

The paper crinkles between my fingers as I walk through the precinct and into the waiting room. Pushing open the door, I call out the name crumpled within my fist.

In response, a young woman stands from the row of orange plastic seats bolted to the floor. She's a thin—*too fucking thin*—beautiful brunette. While she's young, she looks like life has repeatedly kicked her while she was down.

As she approaches, I note the remnants of mascara that have trailed down her cheeks and her messy bun of still-wet hair. Both clear signs that she tried to clean herself up before coming to the station. Her clothes are still those of a woman who was out on the town last night— a tight denim mini skirt and a low-cut tank top that accentuates her cleavage.

"I'm Detective Michales," I extend a hand to her as she approaches. "Why don't we go to one of the interview rooms so we can talk in private."

She gingerly shakes my hand and nods. We walk in silence to the room at the end of the hall, where I offer her one of the cold metal chairs before taking one for myself.

I gather basic details of her alleged assailant before diving into her recollection of events. At least if she becomes a blubbering mess, I'll have height, weight, and hair color for my report.

"Start from the beginning, Mia." I place my notebook on the table between us and lightly tap my pen on it. "Every little detail you can remember. Even if it seems insignificant, it might be useful. Okay?"

Her throat bobs, and her recollection of the evening begins to spew from her in broken fragments that are going to be useless to me.

"So, you agreed to meet Sam after you closed up the bar?"

"Yes." She dips her chin, and a bitter look spreads across her face. "I didn't expect...I...I didn't ask for this."

"I didn't say you did, ma'am." My eyes drop to her practically exposed tits before returning to her face. "What happened when you went outside?"

"He was nice. Sweet. We kissed a bit." She pauses briefly, and I catch a hint of shame in her eyes. "Then he went down on me."

"He performed oral sex on you?" I question to clarify.

"Yes."

"Consensually?"

Closing her eyes, she nods as she replies, "Yes. At first. He wouldn't stop. After I came, he kept going and talking about how good I tasted."

A brief mental image of her splayed across the bed of her truck and being eaten as a meal causes my cock to twitch.

And what kind of woman complains about getting too much head? It's normally them complaining that a man won't go down on them.

"When he finally stopped, he pinned me to my truck and used a bottle..." Her words trail off as though she is too ashamed to continue.

"He used a bottle to what?" The words spill from me with an unprofessional enthusiasm. This isn't the normal run-of-the-mill date rape shit that happens around here.

*This is one of **them**.*

One of those rich assholes related to all those disappearing girls.

Her eyes drop to the table, and she picks at her well-worn cuticles before answering, "To fuck me and bottle my cum. This is all so fucking embarrassing."

"And then?"

"He took what he wanted"—she shifts in her seat and covers her arms across her body—"making me come, he fucked me."

I'm fucking certain it's one of them.

"Without your consent?"

"I was crying and screaming for him to stop, if that's what you're asking." Her tone suddenly grows a bit defensive.

I pause and pretend to scribble some notes on my notepad while I wait for her to calm back down.

"And how did you get away after?"

"Get away?" Her brows furrow with confusion. "He just left me there. I mean, after he invited me back to his place for more, he climbed into his expensive-looking car and left."

"Let me get this straight. He performed oral sex on you, with your consent, proceeded to bring you to completion several more times, and then he invited you to come home with him?" I take a deep breath and let out a sigh. "Are you sure you aren't having regret over the events that unfolded?"

"I knew this was a mistake." She abruptly stands from her seat. "No one ever fucking believes girls like me."

"I'm not saying I don't believe you, Mia. It's just unlike any reports I've taken in the past." Pulling a card from my pocket, I slide it across the table. "I'll look into this further, but you aren't giving me much you go on. Rich, good-looking guy, possibly named Sam, in an expensive car. And you don't know if you could pick him out of a line-up."

"Whatever." She swipes the card from the table and storms out of the room.

Sam...Samuel?

Quickly making my way back to my desk, I pull a stack of folders from the bottom drawer. *The investigation that has made me the laughing fucking stock of the department.* I drop it on my desk frustratedly and flip it open, glancing down at the names.

Camryn Waters
Madeline O'Rourk
Paisley Allen
Liv Alden
Elise Allen
Chloe Wilson

Girls, several of which bear a resemblance to Ms. Dillon, all having disappeared from this town in the past couple of years. Flipping the page, I scroll through my list of potential suspects—*all rich assholes that moved to this quaint town around the time these women started going missing.*

My finger trails the paper as I read through the names until I find it.

Samuel Millington

I fucking knew it...

CHAPTER
SIX

SAMUEL

Rolling over, I feel across the massive bed for the brunette beauty, but the bed is empty.

Just a fucking dream...

A really good fucking dream of another round with her based on my firm cock resting against my stomach. I'm about to wrap my hand around my shaft when the phone on my nightstand buzzes.

EDMUND
Did you go slumming it a couple nights ago?

Maybe. What of it?

Loose ties, kid. .

We've talked about this.

I left her better than I found her.

We both know she loved every last fucking second that I kept her coming for me.

Based on her meeting with Detective Asshole, I'm going to disagree.

This shit can't keep happening.

I've told you time and time and again. Liz will take care of anything you want.

I'm going to disagree.

She can't find women who are truly broken for me to take care of.

The ones she finds fake it, but generally not well enough.

Don't get fucking smart with me, kid.

Grant is sick and fucking tired of cleaning up after you.

No one asked him to.

"I can clean up my own fucking mess," I huff and toss the phone onto the bed. "If I ever actually fucking make one."

The phone buzzes again, and I reluctantly lift it from the plush duvet.

Your messes are going to fall on all of us
one day.

Stop being so fucking sloppy.

Whatever.

Go through Liz.

**And start cleaning up your fucking
messes.**

I got it.

They might all be older than me, but I don't know why
they all have to treat me like I'm a fucking child.

Fucking midnight, and now, I'm wide the fuck awake again.

And really fucking pissed off.

I only managed a few hours of sleep before dreams of
that incessant brunette woke me yet again. Knowing I
won't be getting back to sleep any time soon, I toss back
the cover and momentarily shiver when the cool air-
conditioned breeze hits my naked skin. I slide from the
bed and forgo clothes. My bare feet pad along the hardwood floor as I make my way to the kitchen.

I open a cabinet and grab a glass, filling it with water
from the refrigerator. After drinking it in a single gulp, I
place the empty glass on the counter before reopening
my phone. My thumbs slide over the screen as I scroll
through my contacts. I pause briefly on Liz's name
before continuing to scroll.

I need a girl.

MADAME
I've told you not to text me here.

And I told you I need a girl.

$10K and open for anything.

The usual?

You know what I like.

But blonde this time.

A moment passes before the next message arrives, this one a photo. *Of exactly what I'm looking for.* The blonde woman in the photo is exquisite. So fucking gorgeous that she could grace the cover of a thousand magazines.

I want her until I say I'm done.

$50,000 for the week.

Until I'm done with her.

$100,000/week and she's yours.

Sending the money now.

Delivery address?

My place.

Cora will be a few hours.

Maybe morning.

Let me know.

And I will be wanting her back at some point.

Leaving my phone on the counter, I head to the gym to go a few rounds with the punching bag. My need to release aggression may be what led to my request for her, but I don't want to take my anger toward Grant and Edmund out on her.

I'm going to be so fucking good to her.

Slamming my fists into the heavy bag hanging before me, I pound into it as though I were releasing every bit of my anger on Grant and Edmund until sweat beads over my naked body. Heavy, exhausted breaths spew from me as I slump against bag. Hugging it for support, the faces of all the women in my life flash through my thoughts. All of them so unwilling to be loved.

Charlotte.

Lily.

Amanda.

She's going to be different.

CORA

Madame
You have a job.

When?

A driver will be there to pick you up in two hours.

It's open-ended.

Open-ended?

He wants you for a few days to a few weeks.

He's more than willing to pay.

Any particular interests I should know of?

He's rough.

How rough?

$60K for the week rough.

I gulp after reading the words, both in hesitation and excitement. That is a lot of fucking money. More than anyone has ever come close to offering for a week of my time.

I've had guys smack me around for a whole lot less.

Fuck, most of the time, that's been for free.

Is that going to be a problem?

No. No problem.

Good.

This one gets whatever he wants.

Understood?

Yes, Madame.

Sliding from the bed, I head to the closet and grab a small suitcase. Based solely on the amount of money on the table, I begin pulling modest, upscale clothes from the hangers. *In the event he intends to take me out, I want to be prepared.* When finished, I could easily blend in with the uppity Wall Street wives visiting the Hamptons for the weekend.

Sliding open my dresser drawer next, I top off my clothes with undergarments more suited for a seedy strip club.

These rich old men might like us to blend in, but this is the fantasy they're paying for.

Once packed and showered, I rummage through my remaining lingerie. The weather being too hot to mess with stockings, I opt for a strappy, black, silk and lace, garter-less panty set. Lifting a teal A-line dress from the bed, I slip it on and pull the zipper up the back before pulling on a pair of black stilettos with red soles.

As I'm taking a quick glance in the mirror, the doorbell rings.

"It's open," I shout, knowing that it's the driver to collect me. As I make my way toward the foyer, the driver wheels my suitcase to the car. I follow behind and slide into the backseat.

After an hour of driving out into the country, I finally see signs of civilization ahead. I read the sign as we enter a town that I can only think of as the Hamptons of the south.

Adelaide Cove

The town is vastly divided into townies, who have lived here for decades, with their quaint homes and the sprawling estates of the rich and famous who have descended upon their once adorable little town.

We slow along a tall, stone wall and turn into a short drive before we are stopped at an iron gate. In the distance beyond, is a massive mansion. From the looks of it, sixty thousand dollars is a drop in the ocean for a week of entertainment for this man.

The driver mumbles something into the speaker box, and the gates slowly part to allow us entry. The home before us only grows seemingly more enormous as we approach.

This is so much house for one person.

You'd think a whole family lived here.

We pull to a stop near the front steps. My door opens, but it isn't the driver. Instead, it's a tall, broad-shouldered man with a buzz cut and gorgeous chestnut-colored eyes. He's much younger—*and better looking*—than most of the men who pay for my time and attention. He extends his hand to help me from the car, and I graciously accept.

"It's nice to meet you, Cora." He gently lifts me from the car while awaiting my name.

"And you as well..." I smile broadly as I stare up at him. He towers over me, he must be a solid foot taller than me.

"Samuel." He beams down at me before turning his attention to the driver carrying my bag to the steps. "I'll bring that inside."

Nice.

Polite.

Fucking gorgeous.

What the hell does this man need an escort for?

Is this some sort of Pretty Woman gig?

His hand on the small of my back, and the other carrying my suitcase, Samuel leads me up the steps and into the house. Pausing to place the bag on the floor and shut the door, he continues to usher me just beyond the foyer before he grips my hand.

"Let me get a look at you." He lifts it into the air, turns me back toward him, and glides his eyes over my body. His gaze is hungry, and I know what he's truly asking. Reaching for the zipper at the back of my dress, I slowly undo it. I slip the fabric from my shoulders and let the dress fall to my feet.

"Good girl." His voice is suddenly a bit deeper and gravelly as he stalks around me, inspecting what he's getting. His eyes devour every inch of me as he continues to circle me. "You're fucking perfect, but are you worth what I'm paying for you?"

"Every penny." I meet his unwavering gaze.

"Show me."

SAMUEL

Pulling Cora's hand toward me, I place her palm over my cock, and she grips my already hardened length through my pants. Sliding her hand along me, she kneels at my feet before pressing her lips to my pants. Her lips and teeth tease along the outline of my shaft as she takes her time undoing the zipper of my pants.

Reaching through the hole, she pulls my cock out and wraps her lips around my tip. She takes her time. Working her mouth up and down my length, she lightly fists what doesn't fit in her mouth.

"Deeper," I growl down at her. "I want to feel you gagging as I slide down your throat."

Doing exactly as she's told, she slides me over her tongue and forces me to the back of her throat.

Fuck, she feels good.

Continuing to set a moderate pace, she repeatedly takes me deep, her lips kissing the skin at the base of my shaft.

"Eyes on me." I lightly lift her jaw to draw her attention up to my face. Her eyes meet mine when I slip my fingers into the hair at the back of her head and gather it in my fist. "Don't fucking blink as I fuck your throat."

Without a pause, I forcefully shove my length down her throat. I stare into her eyes as I roughly thrust into her mouth.

Excitement. Arousal. Lust.

And there it is...fear.

Pulling out, she gasps violently for the air that I was depriving her of.

I press my cock to her lips, and she opens wide for me to use her again. Tears stream down her cheeks, and drool drips off her chin from gagging around my length, but I continue to fuck her throat and starve her of air. Sliding in deep, I stare down at her unwavering, yet slightly disoriented, gaze while holding her around my cock. "Fuck, you suck like such a good little whore for me. Do you enjoy being used like you're nothing?"

I'm about to pull out to allow her the opportunity to answer when the doorbell rings.

"Come in. It's open," I shout toward the door as Cora attempts to pull herself off my cock. Fisting her hair hard enough to cause her to wince, I shove myself back into her mouth. "I didn't say you were done, love."

Her eyes dart to the doorway and Grant, who is rapidly approaching, before returning to me where they belong. Her pulse is so fucking rapid; it throbs against my cock.

"I can feel your fucking heart racing as I shove my cock down your throat. Are you scared? Or maybe excited about having him fuck you, too."

The look of fear in her eyes only fuels me, and I drive down her throat even harder than before as I growl, "Two powerful men, using and abusing you like the dirty little whore you are."

Tears stream down her face as she struggles to breathe between my thrusts. I'm so engrossed in her that I don't realize how close Grant has gotten until his hand is firmly wrapped around my throat.

Using his momentum and grip, he pulls me from Cora as he drives me backward into the wall with a thud that forces the air from my lungs. I gasp for air, much like Cora lying on the floor where she fell. Grant shoves his forearm across my chest and uses the entirety of his weight to hold me in place before turning his attention back to Cora.

"Get the fuck out," he yells. "Because when I'm done with him, I guarantee he'll be taking it out on you if you're still here."

I'm unable to speak with Grant pressed so tightly against me, and I'm unable to protest as Cora grabs her dress and scrambles toward the door. Watching my perfect little toy run for the door, following his commands instead of mine, I don't see Grant gearing up to hit me until his fist is buried in my gut and causing me to double over. Heaving in breaths, a second blow rattles my jaw.

"I'm getting real fucking sick and tired of cleaning up after you." He grips my shirt, shoves me back into the wall, and wedges his forearm into my throat. Leaning in and cutting off my ability to breathe, he seethes, "This was the last one. Understood? You can fucking rot in jail if you're this fucking careless again."

"You wouldn't," my words are a mere pained whisper, "Because you'll all be there with me."

"Don't fucking threaten me, kid." Grant drives another fist into my gut, it's hard enough that I crumble to the floor. "And remember that dead men can't talk."

Hunched over on the floor and sucking in air, I hear the door slam.

This isn't the end of this motherfucker.

When I scramble to my feet, the engine of his car roars as he pulls away from the house. I race toward the door and grab my keys from the table in the foyer to chase after him.

Climbing into the car, I quickly slip it into drive and tear down the long entryway. While I'm fully intent on chasing him down, I'm surprised when I find myself slamming on the brakes as I pass her.

CHAPTER
NINE

CORA

Roleplaying and acting out outlandish scenarios aren't exactly out of the norm in my line of work, but this definitely takes the cake.

This Daddy caught me shit—or whatever just happened—is weird.

Heels in hand, walking barefoot in the grass along the long cobblestone drive, I'm startled by a large, black SUV barreling toward the open gate. Not far behind, I can hear the hum of a loud sports car rapidly approaching. It whizzes past me, and the brake lights immediately light up as the tires squeal to a stop.

When I reach the car, the passenger window is down, and I immediately take note of Samuel's bloody face.

"Get in the car." His tone is gruff.

This might be too much—*even for me*—so I hesitate to do as he commands.

"I'm not fucking done with you," he growls as he climbs from the car and stalks toward me.

"Actually, I think you are." I continue walking. Taking a step to walk around him, he firmly grips my hair and pulls me back to him with such force that I hiss in pain, "Fuck."

"I'm still fucking hard." His large hand wraps around my throat, and he squeezes firmly as he grinds himself against my ass.

Trying to push away from him, I grunt, "And I don't see how that's my problem anymore. I think we're done here."

I can play his game.

He has made it beyond obvious that he likes to be in control.

The control.

The forcefulness.

The need for power.

A heads-up on his kinks would've been helpful.

I would've played less willing from the beginning.

Samuel pivots slightly and shoves me forward. My hands crash into the side of his car as I attempt to catch my balance. His body is immediately against mine, pressing me firmly against the hot, sunbaked metal. Warm breath blows against my neck as his hands fumble between us.

He pulls the modest slit at the back of my dress until he tears the seam clear up to my waist. The warm, summer air blows across my now bare ass as he continues to fiddle between us, undoubtedly undoing his pants. "You don't get to suck my cock and walk away like a fucking tease."

"We aren't doing this." I push back from the car—continuing to indulge his fantasy—but he shoves me forward and holds me forcibly in place as he kicks my feet wide.

Shoving himself into me, he groans against my neck, "You're going to take my cock in this soaked cunt of yours, and you're going to fucking love it."

He's so fucking thick. I wince and whimper in pain as he aggressively stretches me. Even through the pain, I can feel him blissfully sliding along my walls. So good I nearly forget about protection, and I blurt out, "Samuel. Condom."

"No fucking chance." He continues to thrust vigorously into me. "I know what you feel like now."

"Samuel," I try to protest, but I grunt his name instead as he bottoms out inside of me.

I would fight him harder, but I fuck enough men to take precautions against getting pregnant. And the boss requires regular testing of her clientele, so the chances of him not being clean are beyond very slim.

"I fuck you bare," he grunts between thrusts, quickly forcing me to the brink. "You feel... too fucking good. And I want... to feel.. every bit.. of you clenching ...around my cock ...when you come."

He drives into me painfully hard from behind, and I claw at the hood of the car as he draws an orgasm from me. It rattles my entire body, and the muscles in my legs tremble so hard that him holding me up is all that keeps me standing. As I'm riding out my wave of bliss, he grips my thigh and hoists it to the side, opening me wider, allowing him to thrust even deeper into me.

"This tight little cunt of yours is fucking perfection around my cock." His lips trail along my neck as he changes his pace, the short, rapid thrusts becoming long, deep ones. His words are muffled against my neck as he continues to slide himself in and out of me, but I faintly catch the words, '*mine*' and '*now*.'

"You fucking love my cock, don't you?" He maintains his deep, languid strokes as he whispers against my ear. Each one brings me closer to coming again, brings both of us closer to coming.

"Yes," I moan as tingling pleasure shoots through me as another wave of euphoria hits me.

It's not a lie. His cock is long, thick, and he knows how to use it to fucking perfection.

I can't fathom why he's buying entertainment.

Women would eagerly fall at his feet to be fucked like this.

His hand wraps around my throat, and he pulls my back to his chest as he continues the slow, deep strokes of his cock. Tilting my face up toward his, he kisses my lips, and tries to press his tongue between them. Regardless of how good he feels, I hesitate because I don't kiss my clients.

"Don't fight me, love." His lips vibrate against mine.

"Sa—" I begin to say his name when he tenderly pushes his tongue over mine. The strokes of his tongue match the pace of his cock as he claims my mouth. It's so deep and passionate that I can't help but melt into it and kiss him back.

For a mere moment, he doesn't feel like a client.

This is not how this job is supposed to go.

Our tongues dancing together, I feel him grow more rigid inside of me. His thrusts quicken as he works toward release. I whimper into his mouth as another orgasm leaves me like putty in his arms causing me to clench around him.

A rattled groan rises from his chest as his hips sputter, and he empties himself inside of me. Staying buried deep in my pussy, he pulls back from our kiss, leaving his lips resting against mine. His words a breathless mumble when he finally says, "You aren't like the others, are you? You're going to let me take care of you."

CHAPTER
TEN

CORA

A gentle rapping of knuckles on my bedroom door wakes me. The tapping starts again, and it's incessant, thwarting any chance I have of managing to get more sleep. Tossing in the bed, I catch a glimpse of the alarm clock.

Fucking eight a.m.

"Cora," a deep, yet soft, voice calls from the other side of the door.

"What?" I groan. Samuel kept me up until well after midnight, and it's way too fucking early for another round.

The knob turns, and the door cracks open barely an inch. "Can I come in?"

It's your dollar, dude.

"Of course." I slide my back up the pillows, quickly smooth my hair, and try to wipe any remnants of sleep from my eyes before he steps inside.

"Good morning." Samuel steps through the threshold. He's dressed significantly more casually than I've seen him in the past couple of days. But the jeans and T-shirt he is wearing fit him way too well to be anything but designer. Bespoke designer at that. They accentuate the broad shoulders and massive muscular physique you'd expect of a professional athlete, or former in his case. Yet, they aren't loose or baggy. They fit as though they were literally made for him, and he looks good.

Nearly as good as when he's not wearing any clothes.

"May I?" He gestures to the bed beside me and waits for a nod before taking a seat. His fingers slide along my jaw, and he smiles at me as he tucks a stray tendril of hair behind my ear. "God, you're fucking gorgeous."

He continues to stare at me like I'm some sort of master-piece. With my morning breath, splotchy skin, and—*I can only assume*—makeshift smoky eye from yesterday's liner I didn't bother to remove before bed, I am definitely no Mona Lisa.

"Come on." He smirks though his tone is serious as he taps my outer thigh. "Time to get up and enjoy the day."

"You're one of those." I feign dramatics and roll my eyes.

"One of those?" he chuckles.

"Yes. Those morning people."

Of which I definitely am not.

"Up. You'll have fun." He smiles as he stands from the bed. "And there will be coffee."

Shamelessly, I can't take my eyes off his rock-hard ass as he walks toward the door. Glancing over his shoulder when he reaches the threshold, as though he could feel my eyes on him, he shoots me his million-dollar smile.

"I'll give you thirty minutes to get ready." He begins to pull the door shut.

"That's not nearly enough ti—" I attempt to rebut the short length of time before he cuts me off.

"Thirty minutes, or I'll be back in here to drag you downstairs kicking and screaming."

There is a strange tinge of truth in his words, and I almost don't doubt that he would follow through. I believe it enough that I forgo washing my hair and opt to pull it into a messy bun to save time.

Samuel is waiting in the foyer by the steps; his eyes fixated on his watch as though he is literally counting down the seconds until my thirty-minute deadline is over.

"What's so important that you're pushing me out of the front door before nine a.m.?" I half-joke as he places his hand on the small of my back and leads me toward the car already parked out front.

"You'll see."

He drives fast through town, almost recklessly, before pulling to a stop outside a small, upscale boutique. He climbs from the car, opens my door, and helps me to my feet.

"I'll go grab us coffee. You head inside and get started."

"Get started?" I can't hide the confusion in my voice as he gestures toward the boutique.

Looking at the door, I notice the 'closed' sign hanging in the window. I'm about to say something when a very well-put-together woman opens the door with a smile that screams she works for commission.

I've met her type before.

"Mr. Millington." She smiles at him a little too hard before dipping her head as she addresses me. "Cora. We've laid out a few things for you, but the store is all yours for the next couple of hours."

*Jesus, this really **is** some Pretty Woman shit.*

"I'm not taking no for an answer." Samuel stops my attempt to decline before I even get a chance to open my mouth. "Whatever you want. And I expect it to be plenty by the time I get back with your coffee. Black, two sugars, right?"

"Y...yes," I stammer, not sure whether I'm more caught off-guard by the shopping spree or the fact that he remembered how I take my coffee.

A girl could get used to being treated like this.

CHAPTER
ELEVEN

SAMUEL

Returning with coffee, I am pleased to find Cora doing exactly as I asked when I step inside the boutique.

"Oh my God, finally!" Cora exclaims when she sees me.

"Did you miss me, love?" I jest as she grabs a cup from my hands and takes a huge swig before realizing her mistake.

"Ugh." Her face distorts in utter disgust, "That's yours. So much cream and sugar—it's a crime to call that coffee."

Extending my hand, she eagerly swaps cups with me before chugging a few gulps from her cup. Cup in hand, she proceeds to look through numerous dresses, skirts, and blouses the staff are bringing her and those hanging around the edges of the store.

"This dress," she swoons as her fingers run over a bright pink slip of fabric. "I absolutely love this cut, but the fuchsia is a little flashy. Does it come in any other colors?"

"I'm sorry, miss," the salesgirl closest to her answers as she smooths the fabric. "This dress is haute couture. The entire collection only comes in this Persian rose."

Fucking women's fashion.

"That's too bad," Cora sighs before moving on to another rack of dresses. Even as she continues to shop, her eyes repeatedly glance back toward the hot fucking pink dress.

She chooses a few more items from the selection, and while she tries to protest, I ensure she gets coordinating bags and shoes for each of them.

"What do you think of this?" I lift a black silk and lace teddy from the table in front of me and hold it up for Cora to see.

"It's beautiful." She steps toward me to touch it.

"You should try it on." I tip my head toward the fitting room at the back of the boutique. "Make sure it fits."

Taking it from me, she makes her way through the store and disappears behind a large rack of dresses. After waiting a moment, I garner the attention of the two ladies working the counter, "Here's my card. Would you mind boxing everything up while I check on her?

"Of course, sir."

I slip to the back of the store and let myself into the fitting room with Cora. She lets out a tiny, adorable gasp when she sees my reflection in the mirror. It's followed by an even more adorable, staggered exhale as she watches me close the door.

"You look fucking gorgeous in that, love." My eyes rake over her body. Her tits and ass on display as the remainder of the lingerie hugs every bit of her as though it was made for her body. "It's such a shame that I'm going to completely destroy it when I tear it from your body."

"Samuel!" she exclaims in a whisper, "You wouldn't dare. This is way too expensive to ruin."

"And you're way too fucking beautiful to have anything keep me from worshipping every inch of your skin." Lightly gripping her hips, I pull her toward me before roaming my fingers along the silk covering her stomach.

God, I fucking need to be inside her.

She tentatively retreats as I continue to step closer to her until her back is pressed against the full-length mirror hanging on the wall. Taking another step, my chest is so close to hers that her tits press into me with every excited breath she takes.

I pull one of her hands over her head and pin it to the cool mirror before grabbing the other and doing the same. She stares up at me, her eyes glimmering with nervous excitement. And that intoxicating, familiar tinge of fear from the two of us getting caught.

Fuck, I love this look on her.

Holding both her wrists in one of my hands, the other is immediately on her throat. Squeezing gently, she lightly moans as my lips and tongue trail along her neck and over her shoulder. I want to taste every inch of her exposed skin.

Continuing down her collarbone, I take my time enjoying the heaving swell of her breasts. Sucking and nibbling on them causes faint whimpers to tremble over her lips. Lips I need to have.

Crashing against them, I'm pleased when they eagerly part for me. My tongue swipes against hers, delicately at first, until my need to consume her becomes nearly unbearable. I plunder her lips, swallowing her faint cries and moans.

Grabbing her thighs, I lift her, and her legs wrap around my waist as my body pins her against the cool mirror behind her. She squeezes her thighs and grinds her hips into me as I continue to claim her mouth.

That sweet cunt of hers can't get enough of me.

Pulling back, I continue to kiss her as I speak, "If I fucked you fast and hard, do you think I'll be able to fill that tight little cunt of yours before we get caught?"

Her heavy breaths vibrate against my lips, as she tries to catch her breath enough to answer me.

"Everything okay in there?" A sweet voice follows a gentle knock on the door.

"Yes. One of the clasps got stuck, and she needed a hand," I call through the door as I release Cora's legs from my waist. Still panting, she slides down my body and the mirror until her heels reach the floor. I dip my head and place a feathered kiss against her ear; I whisper, "I guess we'll never know."

CHAPTER
TWELVE

SAMUEL

"How are things going in here?" I poke my head into the room I've provided Cora with. Between a shower to clean up and taking time to put the things I bought her earlier away, she's been in here for a couple of hours.

"Yes. I'm nearly done." She turns and flashes a coy smile in my direction before returning to the items she's folding and placing neatly into one of the dresser drawers. "These things—they're gorgeous—but you really don't need to—"

"Things are not nearly as gorgeous as you," I mutter under my breath, more to myself than her.

This room has been her safe space since she got here. A place she can retreat to between the time we spend together, the majority of it has been with me inside her. It isn't where I want her—in a room by herself, on the other end of the house from me. But I'm determined that she's going to be different.

She won't be like the others.

"I've told you, I want you to make sure you have everything you need to make yourself at home. I want you to be comfortable here as my guest."

Because you're going to be here for a while

"Your guest." Her voice holds a hint of sarcasm as she lightly ticks up the corner of her mouth before she jests, "A guest with free use of her cunt."

"Don't." My voice is deep and my tone flat as anger heats the back of my neck a deep shade of scarlet. I quickly cross the distance between us. Towering over her, my chest heaves, and I attempt to regain my composure before saying anything further.

She stares up at me, and there is no mistaking the glimmer of fear in those grayish-blue eyes of hers. Even if it wasn't in her eyes, I can smell it. It wafts off her like fucking pheromones—*making her fucking irresistible.*

Fuck, Samuel.

Reel it back in.

You've managed to keep that part of you at bay since she got here.

Closing my eyes and taking a deep breath, I open them to find her swallowing hard as she continues to stare up my chest. Lightly gripping her chin, I tip her face to the side and place a chaste kiss against her jaw.

My eyes locked on hers, I wrap my hand around her slender neck. I squeeze with a firm, yet breathable, grip, force her against the wall and pin her to it.

"I like my women sweet, with a hint of innocence." I slide my cheek along hers until my lips are against her ear before continuing in a deeper, authoritative whisper, "Not with the trashy mouth of a dirty fucking whore. Understand?"

When she doesn't answer, I squeeze her throat a little tighter. Her voice trembles slightly as she responds, "Yes. I understand."

"That's a good girl." I pull back just far enough to place another kiss against her lips. Releasing her neck, I pause to sweep her hair from her face and can't help but stare at her for a moment.

She's so fucking gorgeous.

"Change of plans. I want to take you out."

"We just got home," she rebuts, and I don't address her backtalk because she called it 'home.'

I fucking love the way that sounds.

"I want to talk where I can't wind up fucking you. So I can actually get to know you a little better." I walk to the door before turning back to face her. "Get dressed for me. A sundress. The long, loose floral one."

No one says I can't have a little fun while I get to know her.

In my room, I quickly change into something more suitable before heading downstairs to wait for her in the front sitting room. Only a few minutes later, her heels click down the stairs, and I stand to meet her. The fabric of her dress sways with each step she takes, delicately displaying her curves beneath it.

"You look absolutely stunning." I outstretch my hand to her when she reaches the bottom few steps. "I look forward to showing you off."

She smiles sheepishly in return before mustering a bashful, "Thank you."

Without releasing her hand, I walk her to the car and help her into the passenger seat. I drive us across town to a local vineyard.

"Good afternoon, Mr. Millington," the sommelier greets us when we walk into the tasting room. "And Miss..."

"Cora Durant." She smiles and extends her hand to shake his.

"Any guest of Mr. Millington's is always more than welcome."

They exchange pleasantries for a moment before he returns his attention to me. "I took the liberty of having my staff pull a couple of bottles from the reserve collection for you. Would you like your normal private tasting room?"

"Not today." I slip my hand into Cora's and lace our fingers together. "It's a beautiful day, and I think we'd like to enjoy it on the veranda."

"Of course, sir." He gestures toward the door at the back side of the room. "We'll bring everything out to you promptly."

Squeezing Cora's hand lightly, I give a gentle tug to pull her closer as I walk her outside. We take seats in opposing Adirondack chairs overlooking the luscious landscape of the vineyard.

"This is absolutely beautiful." Cora stares over the view as I remain entirely fixated on her. She blends seamlessly into this world, fitting in like this is the class she was born to be a part of.

"Yes," my eyes continue to roam over her, "absolutely perfect."

"You know you don't have to do that, right?" She glances at me over the small table that separates the two of us.

"Does it make you uncomfortable?" I ask. "To know that I want more from you than a wet cunt or a tight ass?"

A slight rose of blush creeps over her cheeks, and her eyes dip to her lap. Looking up at me through her lashes, her voice is soft when she says, "Maybe. Or maybe I'm just giving you exactly what you want."

Don't fucking toy with me, Cora.

CORA

He takes a short, ragged breath, and for a second, I swear his nostrils flare slightly. The faint sign of anger is gone as quickly as I thought it arrived.

"My good, sweet girl," his fingers lightly dust up and down my forearm that's resting on the arm of the chair while we wait for our wine to arrive. He doesn't break contact with me until a waiter arrives with two matching wine flights, needing to place them on the table between us.

We make small talk as we both savor our first glass of wine. I give him what he wants, answering his questions and letting him get to know anything and everything that he wants to about me. All while sugar-coating it a little to play into the innocence he keeps telling me he wants.

It's not hard.

I had a happy childhood, with two parents who abso-lutely adored one another. They are still happily growing old with each other in Kansas, in the same home I grew up in.

I do this shit for the money.

Not because I have to, unlike some girls.

Fucking rich old men for money has been a sugar baby staple for centuries, and I wasn't above a sad lay with a less-than-desirable man from time to time to ensure I could afford some of the finer things in life. It just turned out that I met a woman who gave me the opportunity to make a fuckton of money doing it instead.

The world is full of men like Samuel. Rich. Powerful. And with a complete lack of time to provide a woman the attention that they need to stick around for an actual relationship.

Women like me are easier.

We have no expectations, and we meet all of theirs.

By the time we're halfway through our flight, Samuel has learned so much about me. Question after question, he could probably name every member of my family at this point.

Yet, I know barely anything about him.

"What about you?" I ask before taking a sip of a new glass of wine.

"Come." He signals for me to join him in his seat. This doesn't quite seem like the kind of establishment where sitting on his lap is appropriate, but I'm also guessing that no one would say a word to him anyway.

As I stand between his feet, he taps his thigh, encouraging me to take a seat. He places his wine on the table before lightly gripping my hips and spinning me until my back is to him. His hands slide over my hips and down my thighs, and he slowly begins to lift the hemline of my dress higher and higher as I lower myself onto his lap. My eyes dart nervously, spanning around us to the other patrons, but no one is watching. With the back of my dress just shy of baring my ass, Samuel drags me onto his lap with a slight growl.

Pulling me up his thighs, he splays the fabric of my dress over his lap until it drapes him like a throw. He shifts his weight under me, and I am surprised when I feel his semi-hard cock pressing against me.

"What about me?" He reaches under my dress and between us.

"You haven't told me a thing about you." I nearly choke on my words as he deftly frees himself from his pants.

His ever-hardening length dusts against the bare skin of my ass as he taps my outer thigh and commands, "Lift."

"Samuel," I gulp. "Maybe we should go somewhere a little more private first."

"Lift." His voice deepens significantly, and he painfully pinches my ass, causing me to rise from his lap just as he wanted. Quickly aligning himself with my entrance, he painfully pulls me back down on him. My pussy, not nearly ready to accommodate him, burns with every inch he forces into me. The pain causes me to wince and bite my lip to keep from crying out.

"You're going to need to learn that I know *what* you need." With a breathy growl, he pulls me over the last couple of inches of his shaft until he's buried to the hilt. "And *when* you need it."

The pain between my thighs causes a rogue tear to roll down my cheek. Using the pad of his thumb, Samuel tenderly wipes it away, "I don't want to hurt you, Cora. But you need to let me take care of you, and that means listening when you're told to do something."

I merely nod my head in agreement, not quite knowing how to respond to him.

His fingers play in the loose curls hanging along my back as he takes the glass of Chardonnay from my hand. After placing it on the table, he pulls me backward until I'm resting against his chest with his cock still inside of me, unmoving.

"You're so fucking perfect when you listen. Sitting so still on my cock in front of all these people. A dirty little secret. **Our** dirty little secret."

As though someone flipped a switch, Samuel's entire demeanor changes, and he's completely soft again.

Except his cock.

In the past week or so, he's flipped on and off countless times. I would worry about Samuel, but I'm almost certain he's absolutely harmless. I've been with violent men before – the kind that needs to smack the shit out of you to feel like they are in control and not to feel small. And he's not like any them.

He's...sweet.

His tone soft, he kisses along the back of my shoulder and asks, "Now, what did you want to learn about me? I'll tell you anything. And when you know enough, I'll take you home and apologize thoroughly for hurting you."

We talk about him for a little over an hour, his cock deep and rigid inside of me the entire time. The stories of his childhood are nowhere near as sweet as mine, but he shares them with me regardless.

With a drunk mother and an abusive stepfather, it's a miracle he is as tender as he is. How football was his escape, a way for him to deal with his feelings and let out the aggression from his home life. He never expected it to become such an iconic part of his life.

Apparently, being riddled with trauma and anger really paid off for him.

"This is hard for me," he professes.

"Sharing?" I clarify.

"This." His hand moves between the two of us. "Wanting this tenderness with you. And needing to fuck you so hard"—*his cock twitches inside of me*—"that you have no choice but to scream and cry for me."

And just like that, he's flipped the switch again.

CHAPTER
FOURTEEN

SAMUEL

"Who says you can't have both?" Cora flirtatiously glances over her shoulder.

Me.

No woman has or will love the vile wickedness inside of me. Not when they actually see the true depths of my darkness. Cora hasn't seen what I actually am—*what I'm trying so desperately to hide from her.*

"You don't have to hide from me, Samuel."

But I do, love.

"Up," I give a gentle nudge of her hip, and she lifts just enough for my cock to slide from her warmth. Reaching beneath us, I tuck myself back into my pants before helping her up from my lap, ensuring that her dress fully covers any of her that might be exposed.

No one else gets to see what is mine.

Cora steps to me when I stand from my seat, and she slides both of her hands up my chest. Lowering my face, I'm met with her deep blue pools staring up at me.

"Let me give you what you want." She presses up onto her toes and stretches toward my ear. Lowering her voice, she whispers, "Make me scream for you. Take me so hard that I cry for you."

"You don't know what you're asking." My cock throbs as I momentarily fantasize about shoving her to the ground and cinching my belt around her throat.

Her soft hair brushes along my jaw as she lowers back to her heels, her gaze unwavering when she meets mine again. Sliding her hands along my chest and down my arms, her touch is so light that she's like a breeze blowing against my shirt. When her palm reaches mine, she slips her fingers into mine.

I want to take everything she's offering.

And so fucking much more.

"Fuck it."

I can get what I need without hurting her.

She will be different.

Without another word, I pull her along the veranda until we reach the employee entrance to the cellar. She struggles to keep up as I take the steep concrete steps, pulling her behind me. As soon as I reach the bottom, I turn to quietly shush her when I hear a small group of customers on a tour. Squeezing her hand, I drag her between a row of barrels and tuck us into the corner behind them.

"Not fucking a sound," I whisper as I place my finger to her lips. She gives a small nod in acknowledgment, and I take my time sliding my finger along her mouth until the tip is resting against her pouted lower lip.

"Open." I mouth the word as I press it between her lips and onto her tongue. Her mouth circles my finger and sucks it lightly as I repeatedly slide it over the length of her tongue.

So fucking eager.

Gripping her jaw, I add two more fingers and begin to thrust them faster and deeper into her mouth, repeatedly causing her to gag lightly. Relishing in her discomfort as I watch the tears begin to well her in her eyes.

"Is this what you wanted?" I shove them deep, and she gags hard, clearly fighting back the need to vomit. Her pooling tears now begin to run, causing mascara to trail down her cheeks, and I can't hold back the smile spreading across my face. "Now, lift that dress for me."

My fingers continue to massage her tongue as she gathers the fabric of her flowing skirt. Inch-by-inch, it slides up her legs until I can see the white lace of her thong. Staring at her perfect cunt through the sheer fabric, I slide my saliva-covered fingers from her mouth. I drag them down her neck, leaving a wet trail in their wake, and wrap them firmly around her throat.

Leaning in until there is barely air between our lips, I squeeze tighter around her throat as I slip my other hand between the delicate fabric of her panties. Without giving her time to react, I press my fingers through the lace with ease. I give a swift tug leaving them nothing more than shreds of fabric in my fist.

I squeeze harder around her throat and her pupils dilate from the restriction. The tiny black saucers grow before my eyes as her mouth gapes open. Gathering the saliva in my mouth, I forcefully spit into hers before shoving her panties between her lips and onto her tongue.

"I want you to remember that you asked for this." My words a deep whisper as I slide my hand along her chin, encouraging her to close her mouth. Quickly lowering the zipper, my throbbing cock springs free, and I can't help but groan at the relief from no longer being stuck in the confines of my pants.

As my pants slide down my thighs, I grip the backs of hers and pull her around my waist as I drive her back into the concrete wall. Trapped between the wall and my body, I press into her until I'm buried to the hilt. I pull back and slam into her again and again.

Every thrust is a brutal, yet blissful, assault on her body. Her back scrapes along the cold, coarse wall as I drive into her, and my hips undoubtedly bruise her inner thighs as I repeatedly drive against her. Muffled whimpers tremble from her lips, the wet wad of panties in her mouth the only thing keeping her cries at bay.

"Your tears are fucking beautiful," I breathlessly whisper as I continue to relentlessly fuck her perfect cunt. The pad of my thumb roughly runs along her lower lip before I firmly cover her mouth and nose with my hand. "But you haven't screamed for me yet, love."

Cora's eyes immediately go wide with fear at the realization that she can't breathe, and as she tries not to panic. A fight she quickly loses, her whole body tightening around me as she violently tries to push my hand from her face. Her nails dig into my hand and rake down my arm as she continues to fight for air.

Fuck, her fight feels like heaven.

Her already tight cunt squeezes painfully around my cock—the fear, lack of air, and my cock all drawing an orgasm from her so strong that her entire body convulses against me. My pace is relentless, and she continues to come for me as I loosen my hand.

Free from my hold, she desperately sucks in a deep breath of air as I continue to take her hard and fast. My fingers slide around her throat, but I don't need to squeeze to get what I need. Her muffled screams vibrate against my palm as her cunt clenches around my cock, and there's no holding back. Burying myself into her with a final savage thrust, I unload with a groan, "Fuck."

CHAPTER
FIFTEEN

CORA

Samuel stays buried inside me after he comes. As both of us struggle to catch our breath, he presses a finger between my lips. Taking his time, he hooks it around the wet, ruined panties and pulls them from my mouth. He drops them to the floor, and his tongue promptly takes their place in my mouth.

As much as I try to fight it, I'm unable to hold back the groan that rattles from my lungs and into his mouth.

This isn't like me.

These men are a job. A quick—*usually lackluster*—fuck. In and out. Certainly, no fucking kissing. Absolutely no fucking feelings. Yet, here I fucking am, with Samuel's tongue down my throat—and loving every fucking second of it.

Fuck, Cora.

Vibrating across my tongue, his own groan echoes mine as he slowly pulls back from our kiss. Our foreheads press together; his lips fluttering against mine as we both try unsuccessfully to slow our breathing.

"You really aren't like the others, are you?" His warm, fruit-scented breath blows across my face as he exhales the words.

"The others?" My question is barely a whisper, as I didn't mean to say the words out loud.

"Hey!" a deep voice billows from further down the aisle of barrels. "You can't be down here without a tour."

Samuel quickly lowers me to my feet as the voice begins walking toward us. I'm unable to stifle my groan when he quickly pulls his still semi-rigid cock from me. He pulls at my dress, ensuring it falls to the floor, before beginning to tuck himself back into his pants.

"I'm serious. You can't be down here." The man's tone is stern, and his brows are furrowed when he repeats himself. The now annoyed man turns the corner, suddenly having a full view of us. He glances down to find Samuel pulling at his zipper. A concerned look spreads over his face, and he asks, "Are you okay, ma'am?"

"Trust me," Samuel snarks as he grasps my hand and pulls me from the corner. "She's more than okay." With a dark chuckle, he shoulder-checks the waiter blocking the narrow corridor between the stacks of barrels. The man falters before regaining his balance, quickly pressing himself against the stacks to make ample room for the two of us to pass.

Instead of walking through the tasting room like we entered the vineyard, he pulls me around the back of the building and straight to the parking lot where his car is waiting.

"Don't we need to pay? Or someth—"

"They'll put it on my tab." His tone is gruff, and I opt not to test his most recent sudden mood change.

The ride back to his place is quiet. While he couldn't keep his hands off me or stop doting on me at the vineyard, he hasn't so much as made eye contact with me since he shut my car door. It's the job, beck and call when they want you.

Sweet. Brutal.

Hot. Cold.

It's like a constant flip with his moods.

Reaching the front of his estate, he pulls up to the base of the steps, where the driver left me a few days ago, before coming to a stop.

"I'm going to park the car and make a call." His eyes never glance in my direction. "Go get cleaned up, and I'll be inside in a bit."

Letting myself out of the car, I have barely shut the door behind me when he starts to pull off.

Wham, bam, thank you ma'am.

I chuckle to myself as I head into the house and up to my room, quite eager to take advantage of the lavish bathtub in my ensuite. Stripping off my dress, I fill the tub with hot, sudsy water, I catch a glimpse of myself in the mirror.

Holy shit...

I expected the smudged runs of mascara around my eyes and cheeks, but it's the rest that shocks me.

Deep, red rings wrap around the front of my throat. Sliding my hand over them, and wrapping my fingers around my neck, there is no denying that they mirror where Samuel had his hands no less than an hour ago. The soreness of my back is quickly explained by the numerous tiny scratches covering the skin between my shoulder blades from repeatedly sliding along the rough concrete walls. Even my inner thighs and hips are peppered with the beginnings of bruises from Samuel driving into me over and over with unrelenting force and need.

"I'm going to look like a fucking blueberry by tomorrow." I shake my head and mumble to myself. Turning away from the mirror, I glide my fingers through the bath water to check the temperature before sliding in. I hiss through my teeth when the heat hits the open skin on my back, igniting every tiny scratch.

I take a deep breath, close my eyes, and sink into the warm comfort of the water as I rest my head against the edge. After taking a few deep breaths, I open my eyes. Startled by Samuel leaning against the doorframe, I jump, and I shout, "Jesus fucking Christ, Samuel!"

CHAPTER
SIXTEEN

CORA

"Did I startle you?" he asks with a mischievous grin.

Stepping through the threshold, he takes his time walking toward the vanity between the double sinks. Unlike the Samuel I drove home with, his eyes are fixated on me with every step. He moves to face the mirror and continues to stare at me through the reflection as he slowly removes the cufflinks from his shirt, never breaking eye contact. Dropping them both the marble countertop with a clatter, he turns and begins making his way to the bathtub.

Towering over me, his feet spread wide, He meticulously rolls up his sleeves, exposing both of his muscular forearms as he asks darkly, "Did I break you, love?"

"You aren't exactly gentle," I quip with a smile as he kneels beside the tub.

"Am I too rough for you?"

"No." My voice is soft, and my answer is tentative as I shake my head.

Did I enjoy every moment in that cellar?

Yes.

Do I think he's holding back?

Also, yes.

Something in my gut tells me that I'm just having glimpses of the tip of the iceberg with Samuel. There is a darkness behind his eyes when his fingers are wrapped around my throat—*with my life literally in his hands.*

A darkness I haven't yet decided whether I should be afraid of.

His fingers trail along the deep red rings running along my throat, and the look spreading across his face can only be described as accomplishment. Sliding down my body, his bare arm breaks the surface of the water.

His rough hand lightly grips my tender inner thigh as he parts my legs. He stares at me, diligently watching my reaction as his fingers travel up my thigh. My chest heaves in both anticipation and hesitation—*even as sore as I am, part of me wants more of him*—as he skims along my skin until his fingers are resting beside my pussy.

"Even sore..." His voice trails off as his fingers lightly dust over the slightly swollen lips between my thighs. My breasts rise and fall over the surface of the sudsy water as my breathing becomes increasingly heavy. He rubs the tip of a finger along my entrance, and my breath hitches slightly. "Even sore, you can't deny how your body reacts to my touch."

A feral groan rattles from my lungs as he slips a finger inside of me. He works it teasingly slowly as he tenderly grips my chin with his other hand, "Does this make your sore little cunt feel better?"

"Yes," I groan as he presses against my G-spot while dragging his finger from me.

"Are you going to come?" He continues to slide and curl that lone finger inside of me. Diligently rubbing over the spot that has me gripping the sides of the tub as my release builds in the pit of my stomach.

"I'm so close." The words blow from me in a breathy exhale. He slows his pace, and the release that was so close begins to slip through my fingers. He pulls so far out of me that his fingertip rubs just inside my entrance.

"We both know this is how you want it." He drives back into me with two additional fingers. The sudden stretch causes me to cry out in both pleasure and pain. "I know this is what you really want, isn't it?

"Yes!" I scream, grinding my hips against the unrelenting thrusts of his fingers. Each one elicits pain and bliss in me as my release builds like a ball of electricity in my stomach.

"Tell me you want me to take care of you." He twists and curls his fingers, and my whole body arches off the base of the tub. "And I'll make you come so fucking hard you'll never forget the feel of me between your thighs."

"Please," I pant.

"Please, what?" He adds the firm pressure of his thumb to my clit.

"Take...care of...me." My thighs quiver as he drags me to the brink. Water splashes over the edges of the tub as he finger fucks me with vigor. The electricity in my stomach shoots through my body, my back curving so much that my face falls beneath the surface of the water as a scream bubbles from me.

"That's my girl," he groans, sliding his fingers from me as I push myself back above the water.

"I'm going to enjoy taking care of you." He grips my chin and pulls me toward him. He softly pushes the wet, matted hair from my face, and his lips press against mine as he speaks against them, "And you're going to love letting me use every inch of you for my pleasure. You're going to love being mine, love."

Part of me wants to argue with him. I'm not his. I'm the hired help; literally being paid to be here for his pleasure. Yet, I can't say I haven't enjoyed my time here. Or that I haven't momentarily fantasized as to what this life would be like.

Being his.

Unlike with so many other clients, I don't have to fake and force it with Samuel. I actually enjoy his company.

Conversationally, we mesh, and we can talk about anything and nothing for hours on end. And when it comes to sex...he can fuck.

Holy shit can he fuck.

The ease and comfort of being with him always makes me wonder the same thing, though.

*If he's this fucking charming **and** amazing in bed, why the fuck is he paying for escorts?*

SAMUEL

"I have to fly to Chicago tonight for an alumni event this weekend." I pause in the doorway.

"Okay." Cora nods.

"I'll leave my credit card with you. Use it for anything you need while I'm gone." I pull my wallet from my pants, slide a black card from it, and leave it on the vanity beside my discarded cufflinks. "I expect your things in my room when I get back."

"Sam—"

"I'm not asking." I cut her off. "I want you in my bed with me."

The words escape me as I say them. I don't share my bed with women—*not like that*. I fuck them and discard them; they don't spend the night. Ever.

I know Cora has only been with me for a week—*and I'm paying her to be*—but the idea of being apart from her doesn't sit well with me.   The only reason I'm not bringing her with me is that I need a little time by myself.

*Time to **be** myself.*

Cora hasn't really seen the monster that I am yet. I want to show her, but I'm almost certain that she will run through the door the moment she finds out how roughly I want to use her.

How I can't stop thinking about being deep inside her as she's on the brink of unconsciousness.

This alumni weekend couldn't have come at a more perfect time.   Normally, I despise them, but college campuses are more than full of girls who will allow me to scratch that itch.

This is how I'll do it.

How I can be good for Cora...

...And keep that darkness inside of me happy.

"You don't come while I'm gone. I want your cunt well rested when I get back. Understand?"

"I understand." she agrees with an adorable pout.

***

For the life of me, I will never understand why colleges have these stupid fucking alumni dinners. I do not need to meet the entire incoming team freshman class to continue to support them on and off the field. *I send more than enough money to both.*

The only highlight of this evening so far is the cute little brunette sitting a few tables over. She bears a slight similarity to Mia, only it's clear she has a different social status. Based on her super petite stature, I'd be surprised if she weren't a member of the cheer squad.

She's exactly what I need.

As dinner ends and things become significantly less formal, I continue to keep my eye on her. Mingling throughout the crowd—*my fame is the true reason I get invited to these things*—I ensure that she stays within my line of sight.

When she grabs her small purse from the table and heads toward the door, I promptly excuse myself from the mundane conversation with some new kid for the team. Pushing open the door, I step into the hallway just in time to see her slipping into the stairwell.

Where are you going, little one?

When I get through the door, her heels click a few flights above me. Staying light on my feet to ensure my soles don't click on the metal steps, I take my time following her as I count her steps to gauge what floor she exits on. She pushes on a door, and the faint sounds of traffic tell me my counting was in vain—*she's on the roof.*

Picking up my pace, I take the steps two at a time to get to her. I glance through the small glass pane and she's standing just a few feet beyond the door. A cigarette rests between her lips, and she's rifling through her bag.

Taking advantage of her current distraction, I push open the fire door and snake my arms around her. One around her throat and the other around her tiny waist; squeezing hard, I silence her as I lift her from the ground and carry her away from the door.

"Smoking is a nasty habit," I snicker while using the arm around her waist to pull her skirt up her lean thighs. "Dangerous even."

Garbled screams and cries for help vibrate against my forearm, which is wrapped so tightly around her throat that no sound comes from her.

Too bad...

"You can fight me, little one. I like it. You're going to find out just how much when I make you scream for me."

Undoing my pants, I reach into my boxers and grab my—*flaccid*—cock.

What the fuck?

Gripping it firmly in my fist, I vigorously stroke it against her bare ass. As good as my hand feels sliding over my length, my cock doesn't get hard.

This doesn't happen to me.

Ever.

My virility is generally like that of a teenager, with my cock growing hard practically on command, and the ability to nut is easily there several times a day. More, when surrounded by the right motivation.

"Fuck," I angrily hiss against the girl squirming in my tight hold. Letting go, I shove her from me with enough force that she crumples to the rooftop. Before she has a chance to see my face, I turn and head back to the door. Her faint sobs and cries for help sound behind me, but they do nothing for me.

Her screams aren't the ones I want.

Taking the stairs quickly, I exit a couple of floors above the alumni party and take the elevator down to the lobby. Ditching the party, I head outside and straight to the rental car.

"Fuck, **fuck**, **Fuuuuuuck**," I yell as I pound my fists against the steering wheel.

This weekend was a mistake.

I shouldn't have come here...

...For this.

I know exactly what I want.

And where to find her.

CORA

The phone ringing incessantly on the nightstand wakes me from my sleep. Glancing at the clock on the bedside table, it's late. One in the morning late. After rubbing the sleep from my eyes, I flip on the light, grab the phone and swipe it open.

> **Samuel**
> Are you awake, Cora?

> I need to know...

> Are you being a good girl for me?

> Have you done as you were told?

> > Yes.

> > Everything.

> Are you in my bed, love?

Yes.

Good girl.

Do you like it?

Like it?

Being in my bed?

I do.

It's big and lonely though.

Would you be saying that if I weren't paying you?

The simple answer is the one I know he wants. But with my thumbs resting against the screen of the phone, I hesitate for a moment as I think about my answer. My honest answer. The first rule of this business is that you don't get attached to clients—*because no one winds up like Julia Roberts*—and my answer violates that rule.

I haven't known you long, Samuel.

But yes.

Without the job, it's still a yes.

I would like to get to know you better.

I shouldn't have left you there alone.

I'll be home in the morning.

I thought you had to be gone all weekend?

I wait a moment for a response before sending another of my own.

Samuel?

Still nothing from him. No sign he's responding either.

Are you okay?

Nothing. I wait a few more minutes before flipping the bedside light back off and trying to get back to sleep.

***

"Good morning, beautiful." Samuel's tone is soft as his fingers rub along my jaw.

"Samuel." A smile spreads across my face through my yawn as he wakes me.

"Did you mean what you said last night?"

"About giving us a try?" My words are slow, and my tone groggy as I try to wake up. "Yes. I meant it."

My eyes flutter, fighting the bright morning light, and I vaguely see Samuel towering over me. Forcing my eyes to focus, I realize that he's naked and straddling my chest.

"Good. I want to learn who you really are. I want to take care of you," he grips my hand and pulls it above my head as he reaches for the other, "but I need to show you who I really am."

"Show me," I blurt, part of me is all too eager to see the side of him that he's been hiding.

He holds my hands in place as he slides further up my body until my upper arms are pinned under his shins. He shifts his weight until his cock is resting against my lips. "Open."

Opening wide to accommodate him, he repeatedly taps the soft head of his tip against my lower lip before pausing, "How far are you willing to go?"

"However far I need to"—my words vibrate against the head of his cock—"for you to show me who you are."

Gripping the headboard with one hand and his cock with the other, he presses himself over my tongue and down my throat as he groans, "I'm the reason you live or die."

Using the headboard for leverage, he thrusts into my mouth as he fucks my face. Unwaveringly deep, I gag around him as he repeatedly slams down my throat. Every drive of his beautiful, thick length fills my mouth and throat, growing more demanding with every spasming gag he causes.

My heart pounds, fear sinking in as the urge to take a breath grows; I start to wonder if he has any intention of pulling out far enough to allow me to breathe.

"You feel so fucking good when you're scared, and your pulse is thumping around my cock." He pulls back until he's no longer in my throat, and I struggle to suck in air around him filling my mouth with his thick length. My breaths are still deep and heavy, and he proceeds to slide back over my tongue. "This time, I'm not stopping until you're swallowing every fucking drop I spill down your fucking throat."

His shins dig into my arms, and the headboard rocks as he continues to use it for leverage; his hips repeatedly driving his cock even deeper down my throat. There is nothing even remotely soft about how he's taking me. This is one hundred percent for him, yet my own arousal tingles between my thighs.

No, fucking throbs between them.

Groans and grunts rattle from him as he slams into me, and I gag around his girth. My lungs begin to burn, as my body fights to take a breath that Samuel isn't allowing me to have. Reflexes take over, and my body begins to thrash beneath him, trying to push him from me to save my life.

He quickens his already brutal pace, and my throat tightens around him as I struggle futilely to suck in the tiniest bit of air. My eyelids flutter, and blackness begins to creep over my vision, when he lets out a raspy, guttural groan, "Fuck, love."

My body is exhausted and still on the brink of fading to black the saltiness of his release spurts onto the back of my tongue as he slowly retreats from my throat and mouth.

CHAPTER
NINETEEN

SAMUEL

"You did so fucking good. And, fuck, do you ever feel good when you fight me." I pull myself from between her swollen lips as I climb off her chest. Settling next to her on the bed, I drag her almost limp body into mine without a hint of struggle.

The things I could do to her right now.

So pliable.

So perfect.

Positioning her snuggly into the bend of my hips, I hold her against me and relish in the warm skin of her back pressed to my chest. I kiss along the side of her neck and pause for a moment when I feel her pulse against my lips. It's a soft flutter, slowly growing stronger and more steady with each beat of her heart. I continue down her long neck and over the soft skin of her shoulder as I slide

my hand down the dip in her waist and over the curva-
ture of her hip.

I can smell her sweet scent—*it was all I could focus on as I
claimed her throat as my true self*—but it isn't until I slide
my fingers between her thighs that I feel how absolutely
soaked she is.

"God, you're so fucking perfect." I rub my hand through
the slick sweetness coating her upper thighs. "You're so
fucking wet from being used. You're fucking covered it."

Lifting my hand, I rub her glistening arousal between my
fingers before licking them with a groan.

Always fucking delectable.

Glancing down her body, I note the dark spot on the gray
sheets where she was lying. "So fucking turned on from
being nothing more than a fuck hole that you've soaked
my sheets."

*I've never had a woman get this wet and aroused from being...
taken...used entirely for my pleasure.*

But Cora, her body is telling me everything I need to know.

Even if she isn't lucid enough to say it.

She was fucking made for me.

I slip two fingers inside of her cunt with ease, and she
startles slightly in my hold. Her reaction is still groggy as
she lingers on the edge of unconsciousness, almost as
though she's on the verge of sleep.

"Shhh. You did so good for me, love. Let me reward you for being such a good girl."

Working in and out of her at a slow pace, I repeatedly drag my fingers firmly over the fleshy spot inside her that always causes her to groan for me.

And I get exactly what I want...

Raspy groans rattle through her sore throat, and she sucks in air as she begins to quiver around my fingers. "That's it. Deep breaths for me. Let the air fill your lungs so you can scream for me when I make you come."

Her voice is strained and hoarse when my name passes over her lips in a pained whisper. Whimpers blow from her mouth as she rhythmically clenches around my fingers. Her body arches, pressing her ass into my hips and opening her neck to me.

"That's it, love," I grunt the words against her neck as she becomes more lucid, her body needily reacting to every curl of my fingers inside of her.

Reaching between her thighs, she cups her hand over mine, holding me deep as she grinds against my palm. She comes quiet, yet hard; her whole body going rigid as her thighs tremble and squeeze together around our hands.

"I told you, Cora." I use my free hand to brush her hair from her neck so that I can press my lips to her skin. "I just want to take care of you."

I know that now.

She can give me everything I need.

And I can give her more than she could ever imagine.

We lay in silence, my fingers still lightly massaging deep inside of her, milking every bit of pleasure from her orgasm until the walls of her tight cunt stop quivering. Tenderly sliding from her, I bring them to my mouth to enjoy the taste of her again.

Breaking the silence, Cora's voice is raw, with a hint of humor, when she asks, "Are you going to kill me with your cock, Samuel?"

"Not on purpose." My response is devoid of emotion.

But it's also honest.

I've never killed any of the women before her on purpose. Or at least, I didn't plan to.

Wrapping both my arms around her and holding her against me, I place a kiss on the crook of her neck before continuing. "Asphyxiation is a finicky bitch."

"You're a sick fuck." Her tone is laced with both serious-ness and a hint of dry wit. From her tone, I'm half expecting her to climb from the bed and run for the door. Instead, she shimmies backward as though she needs to remove any distance between the two of us.

"Yes, I am." I throw a leg over her and envelope her with my body. "And you're equally as depraved, love."

CHAPTER
TWENTY

CORA

"What is this?" I try to tone back my excitement when Samuel steps into the room carrying a lavishly decorated black gift box.

Carrying it across the room, he carefully sets in on my lap, and I can't pull my eyes from the ornate box. It's matte black with a black, glossy, paisley design adorning the lid, all of it topped with a silky, white bow. Samuel delicately slips his finger under my chin before lightly tipping it up toward his face, drawing my eyes to his.

"I want you to have everything you've ever wanted." He dips his head and tenderly kisses my lips. "Everything. Things you didn't even know you desired."

Samuel takes a seat on the coffee table in front of me and waits patiently for me to open the box. I pull on the white silk, and the ribbons slide from the box to my lap and the floor.   My fingers linger over the smooth detailing covering the lid as I lift it off the box. Beneath it lies tissue paper with a similar paisley detailing. Peeling it back, I find a dress.

As I lift it from the box, I immediately recognize it as the gorgeous hot pink monstrosity I was eyeing the other day—only it's not that horrid shade of pink. The one I'm lifting from the box is a deep burgundy.

My favorite color.

"Samuel," I gasp in awe of the thoughtfulness of his gift.

"Do you like it?"

"I love it!" I exclaim as I hold it against me. "But...How did you?"

"I saw how disappointed you were, so I called in a few favors," he explains as I carefully lay the dress back into the box. "Everything you could ever want; I'll give to you."

The way Samuel dotes on me is unlike anything I've ever experienced. Things like remembering how I like my coffee, or my favorite color are small; but somehow, the way he presents his knowledge of them feels so mean-ingful. *So not normal for me.* But going to outlandish lengths for this dress.... I don't think I've ever met a man willing to do something like that.

For me or anyone else.

The things he says about wanting to take care of me aren't complete bullshit. He truly wants to. He enjoys it so much that it's almost as though he gets off on spoiling me and making me happy.

Wrapping my arms around his neck, I lean down to kiss him. A soft, tender thank-you kiss that I find myself unable to pull back from. Lingering against his lips, he lightly flicks his tongue between mine, and I don't hesitate to let him in. Our tongues sweep teasingly against one another as we each begin to grow breathless. The kiss between us growing more needy, I climb into his lap, straddling him.

Gripping my hips, he slides me up his thighs and against his hips until I can feel him growing hard beneath me. Using his firm hands to guide me, he grinds me over his length.

"Do you like how I take care of you?" He shifts his weight, sliding me onto one of his thighs. A rigid, muscular thigh that he continues to rub my hips against.

"You spoil me, Samuel." I breathlessly grunt the words as I slide my pussy along the hard bulges of his quad while his hands begin to travel up my spine. His fingers dig into my skin, and I can't stifle the moan that rattles from me.

Slipping his fingers into my hair, I practically melt into his hands as I continue to work myself over his thigh. He takes a fistful of my hair, and he roughly tips my head to the side before sinking his teeth into the crook of my neck.

And there he is, the other side of him.

Samuel is Jekyll and Hyde. Two vastly different men living in the same body. One soft and tender. The other brutal and depraved. He flips between the two of them sporadically.

It's exhausting.

Absurd.

Crazy.

No, Cora.

Crazy is delving into his fantasy, letting it become your own.

His behavior isn't normal. It's unhinged, even. Yet here I am, yearning for more of him.

The sweetness. The darkness. All of it.

Samuel draws back from my neck, and my skin is already tender where he has marked me. He pulls even harder at my hair, forcing me to arch my back and grind down even harder on his thigh.

"Your perfect little cunt is so fucking needy. Soaking my pants and begging for my cock." His voice is deep and gravelly as he stares into my eyes. Standing us both from the table, Samuel roughly drops me face-first onto the sofa, pushing my sundress up my back, and he climbs on top of me.

The familiar feeling of silk dusts over my skin as Samuel slips it under my throat. Gripping the ribbon, he crosses it against my back and yanks it to my hips. Pulling it taut around my throat as he slips inside of me, he growls, "I know exactly what you need."

And it's fucking terrifying how right he is.

CHAPTER
TWENTY-ONE

SAMUEL

Cora's arm and leg drape over me, as her head falls to my chest, and her beautiful blonde locks splay across my shoulder. Both of us are completely spent and beyond satiated. Her sweaty body slips from where she lay, and she falls between me and the back of the couch. Gripping her hip, I carefully pull her back on top of me, and she nuzzles back into me.

I fucking love how she feels against me.

My fingertips aimlessly travel the length of her spine, from the nape of her neck to the adorable dimples just above her ass. In turn, hers trace over ridges and rivets of my chest and abs.

Turning my head, I press my lips to the cool, damp skin of her forehead before breaking the serene silence in the room.

Never have I met a woman who can handle me.

My kinks.

My dark needs.

The depraved enjoyment I get as I watch the light dwindle from their eyes as I fuck them.

When I brought Cora here, I only hoped that she would be different from the women before her. That she would let me care for her the way she deserved—the way I know she needs. But I never imagined how much she would enjoy coming on the literal brink of death.

She's fucking perfect.

"You're a first for me, Cora." I place another kiss as I tighten my embrace, "I've never met a woman quite like you."

"You've never met a foul-mouthed, sarcastic delight before?" she quips as she props her chin into her hands on my chest.

"Plenty," I snark, "but none like you."

"What makes me so special?"

"This." I lay her head back on my chest and continue stroking along her back with light caresses of my hand. "I fucking adore you like this."

"Sweaty and exhausted?" she chuckles. "Or naked in your arms?"

"Both." I give a light swat on her ass for her insolence. "The comfort I feel from just being here with you is like nothing...like nothing I've ever felt with anyone else."

Cora stiffens slightly in my arms, and I think for the first time since she's been here, I might have actually spooked her.

"Relax." I wrap my arms around her tightly to prevent her from getting up. "I'm not going to profess my undying love for you and ask you to become Mrs. Millington."

Although I have no intention of letting her get away from me.

"I like being here too, Samuel." Her voice is soft this time as she settles back against me.

"Good."

As we talk, Cora's words begin to become sluggish, and it's obvious that she's slowly drifting off to sleep. Peppering kisses across her forehead, I continue to soothingly rub her back as her eyelids begin to flutter.

"Go to sleep, love," I breathe the words against her forehead. "You're safe with me."

***

Opening my eyes, I quickly realize that Cora wasn't the only one who was tired. At some point, while staring down at her peacefully sleeping on my chest and listening to the sweet little sounds she makes, I drifted off as well.

Slipping from beneath her, and being careful not to wake her, I grab my boxers from the floor and head to the kitchen. I pull them on as I stand before the cool draft of the refrigerator and pull out a jug of orange juice and a bunch of grapes. I'm in the middle of pouring a glass of juice when Cora pads into the kitchen, wearing nothing but my shirt.

Fucking exemplary.

I can't pull my eyes off her. She's swimming in my shirt, repeatedly pushing the sleeves up as she walks.

"What are you doing?" she asks as she makes her way to the counter. Gripping her waist, I lift her into the air and plop her bare ass on the counter. She squeaks when the icy granite touches her skin.

"Drink," I demand softly before lifting the glass of juice to her lips. She parts her lips, and I tip the glass enough to pour some into her mouth. She attempts to back away, but I continue to pour it into her, "More, love. You need it."

She takes another gulp, and I lower the glass.

"I generally prefer my orange juice over champagne," she smirks as she takes the glass from my hand.

"Next time." I step between her thighs and cup her ass with both my hands. "But right now, you're going to do as I say. Now, open your mouth."

Cora opens her mouth, and I press a grape between her lips. She allows me to feed her a few of them. I place another into her mouth, as she sarcastically says, "I prefer these smushed and a tad fermented."

"Feeling a little bratty, are we?" I cup her chin and kiss her lips. "You won't be able to talk with my cock in your mouth."

"I won't be able to eat either," she quips.

"Touché." I smile and kiss her again. "Now, shut up and eat so you have strength for me later."

CORA

Samuel sure has me fucking figured out.

I'm a sick, depraved fuck.

Maybe all this asphyxiation is causing brain damage, but I can't fucking get enough of him. I glance over my shoulder at him, sitting a few tables behind me at the coffee shop, only to find him staring back at me with an unwavering hunger in his eyes.

Be strong, Cora.

"You are not fucking me in the bathroom of this coffee shop," I mouth the words before turning back to the counter to wait for our coffee order.

My phone immediately buzzes in my pocket, and I know it's him before I pull it from my jeans.

Samuel
I'll fuck you when and where I want.

If I wanted to bend you over the fucking counter, you'd take every fucking inch of me as everyone in here watched what a slut you are for me.

You'd fight me, but you'd love every fucking second of it.

I'm about to put it back into my pocket when it buzzes again.

Maybe I'll get one of these women to eat that perfect cunt of yours while I take your ass.

You seemed to enjoy that yesterday.

Fuck, he isn't wrong...what an afternoon.

Tell me you aren't wet...

Shoving the phone back into my pocket, I turn to find a devilish grin spread clear across his face.

Fucking bastard.

It took him no time at all to figure out exactly what makes me tick—being completely at his mercy. The rest of this relationship thing, we're kind of figuring that out as we go.

"Cora," the barista calls my name and slides two paper cups in my direction.

"Thank you." I nod as I lift them both from the counter. Turning, I immediately notice that the fun, playful look has completely dissipated from Samuel's face. In its place is a dark scowl. Pure, unadulterated anger.

Murderous rage.

It isn't until the woman in front of me moves that I realize a middle-aged gentleman has helped himself to my seat across the table from Samuel. The man has a folder splayed open and is aggressively pointing at the contents, as though he's goading Samuel to look at whatever is laid on the table before him.

The man quickly closes the folder and pulls it back to his side of the table when he sees me approaching. Placing the coffee order before Samuel, I tentatively question, "Everything okay here?"

"Perfect, love." Samuel's response oozes with tension as he stands from his seat.

"I don't think we've met." The gentleman stands as he extends a hand toward me.

"Cora Durant." I hesitantly slip my hand into his.

"Detective Michales," he responds, and I glance to Samuel, my inquisitiveness clearly written across my face. "And how long have you known Mr. Millington?"

"A couple of we—"

"She doesn't need to answer any of your questions," Samuel interrupts me, ire lacing his tone. "If you want to talk to her, you can contact my attorney."

"I'm thinking we enjoy our coffee anywhere but here." Samuel grabs his cup and gently nudges me toward the exit. Grabbing my free hand, he begins pulling me past the detective. Even though I'm unsure of what exactly is happening, I don't resist him.

"You might want to be more selective with the company you decided to keep." The detective firmly grips my arm as I attempt to pass him and my hand slips from Samuel's grasp. His grip is firm and unrelenting when I attempt to pull from him. He shoves a card into my hand as he continues, "If you want to know who he really is, call me."

"Remove your fucking hands from her." Samuel aggressively shoves him. The detective releases my arm, and I immediately rub over the tender spot where he gripped me as I watch the two of them square up. "You don't *ever* fucking touch her. Because I'll fucking kill you if you do it again."

"Did you just assault *and* threaten an officer of the law?" The detective reaches for his hip and flips the strap of his holster off his gun.

The two of them have garnered the attention of every patron inside the small shop as well as a few onlookers from the sidewalk.

"Samuel..." My voice is soft as I timidly grab at his arm. When he doesn't respond, I squeeze a little and repeat his name. "Samuel. We should go."

Breaking his attention from the detective before him, Samuel looks at me, and I gently usher him toward the exit before slipping my hand back into his.

He pushes open the door, and the detective calls after us, "I'll be seeing you soon, Samuel. Probably you too, Cora."

Samuel squeezes my hand firmly as he practically drags me down the street. There is no denying his anger or the distance he is attempting to put between us and the detective.

Glancing down as I struggle to keep up with his brisk pace, I read the business card tucked in between my fingers and the coffee cup.

DETECTIVE MICHALES
Homicide/Violent Crimes

What the actual fuck?

TWENTY-THREE

DETECTIVE MICHALES

Pulling a pen from my pocket, I quickly scribble down Cora's name and a brief description of her appearance.

Cora Durant.
Early twenties, Caucasian, blonde, blue eyes,
no discernible marks.
...actual relationship with SM?

Now, I just need to wait for her to turn up missing—or dead.

It's morbid as hell, but he won't be able to stop himself. And when she's lying on a slab in the mortuary, he won't be able to deny his relationship with her. At least twenty people saw the two of them together. And I did my part. I told her what kind of man she's with. I can't force her to leave him.

She's going to be how I get these assholes.

Leaving the coffee shop, I head to my car parked out front. I climb in and toss Mia's case file on the passenger seat before cutting into traffic to follow Samuel.

I've been tailing him nearly every moment that I'm not on the clock. Approaching him in public isn't exactly normal procedure, but I wanted to rattle him. Needed to, in the hope that he'll fuck up and make a mistake.

CORA

"Samuel, baby," I continue to press as he drives us home at reckless speeds, "Please tell me what the hell is going on."

"It's nothing." His voice is flat, and he still refuses to make eye contact with me.

"Just tell me what that was all about."

"I **said** it's nothing."

Bullshit.

Fucking bullshit.

Reaching between our seats, and hoping to God I don't pull too hard, I wrap my fingers around the emergency brake and lift it a notch. The tires squeal as the brakes lock in place, and the antique sports car begins to fishtail uncontrollably across the road. We slide along the shoulder, loose gravel and dust kicking into the air in our wake.

Samuel regains control and brings the car to a stop, resting half on the road and half on shoulder, before throwing the car into park. Spinning in his seat, his nostrils flare, and his face beet-red with anger when he seethes, "What the fuck, Cora! You could've fucking killed us."

"You don't get to ignore whatever just happened," I practically shout at him. "Because I'm not going to ignore whatever the fuck that was."

Samuel stares at me with narrow eyes, an angry shade of red covering his face as his nostrils continue to flare with every heavy breath he takes.

"You don't get to lie to me." I shake my head as I say the words, "Police detectives don't shove evidence files in your face or give ominous warnings over nothing, Samuel. So don't fucking tell me it was nothing."

"Fuck, Cora!" He slams a fist into the steering wheel before shifting the car back into drive. "We're not doing this here."

"Sam—"

"You're fucking incessant." He cuts me off as he quickly pulls the car fully to the side of the road. Slamming on the brakes and putting the car back into park, his voice is dark. "You want to do this right now? Fine."

"Samuel, just tell me why a homicide detective is hounding you?"

He doesn't answer me, though. Instead, he only stares at me with his dark eyes.

"Damn it, Samuel. Just fucking answer me. Why is he telling me to be careful around you?"

He continues to stare back at me in silence. With a dark, unwavering gaze, he tenderly brushes the backside of his hand along my cheek. His fingers tangle in my hair as he slides them toward the back of my head.

As though his switch flips, he roughly fists the hair in his hand. He pulls so hard that I yelp from the searing pain in my scalp. He yanks again, leaving our faces only inches apart. So close that his hot, angry breath wafts across my face as he breaths. When he finally breaks his silence, his words hit my skin like ice, "You know why."

My breath sputters at his words, and my brain tries to assemble the puzzle before me quickly.

I know.

I think I've always known.

I'm just afraid to admit it to myself.

"You're a killer...A murderer," I exhale. He doesn't deny it in the slightest. Instead, there's a small glint in his eyes.

"How many?" I try to hide the nervous tremble in my voice.

Fuck, Cora.

Don't be stupid. Just get out of the fucking car.

"A few." His tone is flat and devoid of any emotion. My blood suddenly feels as though I have ice water running through my veins.

"Accidents?" I try to rationalize his answer somehow, knowing full well how rough he likes to play.

"A few," he repeats his previous answer and I'm suddenly filled with disgust.

The things I've done for this man.

*The feelings I had—**no, have**—for him.*

"Now," he loosens his painfully tight grip on my hair, "do you think you can refrain from doing anything reckless so I can take us home?"

I silently nod my head in agreement.

"Behave, and we can talk about this later," Samuel puts the car into drive and slips his hand along my thigh. He slides it high enough that my dress is resting along my hips. An hour ago, his touch would've been warm and comforting. Now, it's like an icy talon burning his evil through my skin.

It takes every bit of self-restraint to keep from pushing him away during the ten minutes it takes to get to his estate. Not saying anything, on the other hand, is simple because I suddenly feel like I'm sitting beside a stranger.

A dark, murderous stranger.

My heart pounds as we pull through the iron gates, and my stomach drops when I see them close behind us in the side view mirror.

With Samuel's eyes fixated on the winding drive before us, I try to discreetly slip my heels from my feet. Both are resting beneath me when Samuel pulls to a stop at the front steps.

I undo my seatbelt when he grabs for his door handle but resist the urge to open mine. Samuel always gets my door. I won't make it two feet if he realizes what's happening.

Sliding from the driver's seat and climbing out of the door, I take my chance as his back is to me. Gripping the handle, I throw open the door and spring from the car. Not thinking about how I'm going to actually get through it, I run toward the gate.

"You're being reckless, Cora," Samuel calls after me. The playfulness of his tone is absolutely terrifying, and I fight the need to turn back enough to see whether his face mirrors his enjoyment.

My bare feet scrape across the cobblestone drive as I continue sprinting toward the exit—to safety.

"Fuck, Cora!" Samuel yells. "Don't make me fucking do this." His voice is loud, angry, labored.

And so fucking close.

He hits me from behind, with every bit of force expected from a former NFL offensive tackle. His upper body plows into my thighs, and I crumble to the ground. I hit it with such force that it knocks the wind from my lungs. Startled and breathless, I'm helpless as he climbs on top of me.

His massive body is a giant weight on my back, pinning me to the hard bricks beneath me and forbidding me from drawing in the deep breath of air my body so desperately craves.

This is how it ends for me.

SAMUEL

"What did you go and do?" I press my weight into her back as I breathe the angered words against her ear, "You know you shouldn't have done that."

"Samuel," she grunts my name painfully.

Snaking my arm beneath her, I slide it under her chin and around her until her delicate neck is resting snuggly in the crook of my elbow.

"I was good to you, Cora." I squeeze my arm enough to force her face toward me. "I was so fucking good to you."

Her hands grip my forearm, her nails digging into my skin as she tries to free herself from my hold as I pour my heart into her ear. "I spoiled you. Gave you everything you wanted. I was fucking kind and generous. I gave you parts of me that I've never given anyone."

Fucking ungrateful.

"If this is how you're going to treat me, maybe I was too fucking good to you. Maybe you need to see the part of me I haven't shown you yet."

The fingers clawing at my skin begin to slow and become softer as Cora begins to run out of oxygen. I loosen my grip to allow her to take a breath so she remains conscious. I place a kiss against her ear before whispering, "No, love. I want you awake, so you can see how fucking good I've been to you."

Reaching between us with my free hand, I undo my belt and lower my zipper. My cock—hard from the moment I pinned her to the ground—springs free, and I give it a few teasing strokes before lifting Cora's dress.

My finger slides along the crack of her ass, and I use it to hook her thong. Stroking against her asshole, she jerks her body and tries to pull away from my touch. I pull the thong from between her cheeks, and I yank it to the side and press my tip into her cunt. It's fucking tighter than hell as she clenches hard, trying to keep me from entering her.

"Fuck," I grunt against the back of her neck as I press myself inside of her. "Squeeze my fucking cock. You're so fucking tight, it's like fucking a virgin cunt."

Her fingers and toes claw at the rough ground beneath her. She fights against me, but her body tells a different story. I continue to slide in and out of her, her slick cunt growing increasingly wetter with every stroke of my cock.

"Tight. Wet. And so fucking ready to be pumped full of my cum." I repeatedly slam my hips against her ass. "You fucking love this, don't you?"

Her cunt quivers rhythmically around my cock, and I know she's going to come for me.

Whether she wants to or not.

Flexing my arm, I tighten the hold on her neck as I deepen my thrusts. "You can't fight it, love. Your cunt was made to take my cock. It will always make you come. *I* will always make you come."

Droplets of tears from her face fall to my forearm as her body finally gives in to what she needs. Her cunt clenches around me as her body grows rigid beneath me.

"That's my good girl," I groan into her ear, slamming into her as I continue to deprive her of the ability to breathe. Her body softens beneath me as she teeters on the bridge of consciousness. Not loosening my grip, I drive into her a few more times before filling her perfect cunt. I groan through my release, every blow of cum from my cock better than the last.

Releasing my flexed bicep, Cora's face lolls against my forearm. Gently laying her face against the bricks beneath us, I climb off her limp body and tuck my spent cock back into my pants. I kneel beside her, lift her near-lifeless body into my arms, and begin carrying her into the house. I can barely take my eyes off her. Even with blood and mascara staining her face, she's fucking beautiful.

My perfect little Cora.

As I carry her upstairs and straight to my room, I continue to hold her as I turn on the water to draw a bath. Once the water reaches a comfortable temperature, I lay her on the bathmat to quickly strip from my clothes before helping her from hers.

"You're a mess, love," I mutter mostly to myself. She is covered in blood. It marks her knees and elbows where she ground against the cobblestones as I fucked her the way she needed. Her left cheek has a small gash, likely from taking the brunt of her fall, and blood has crusted along her jaw.

Scooping her back into my arms, I climb the two of us into the tub. I carefully lower us both into the hot water below, and Cora's body startles when it touches her skin.

I pull her tightly to me and sink us both into the water as her eyes dart open.

"Welcome back, love."

CHAPTER
TWENTY-SIX

CORA

Opening my eyes and seeing Samuel—so calm, with gentleness in his eyes again—pressed against me, I open my mouth to scream. I quickly find it covered with his hand, my screams muffled against his palm.

"We aren't going to do that." He squeezes my cheeks with just enough force to cause me to wince. "I let you have your moment. I had mine. Now, you're going to behave for me, and I'm going to put that part of me away from you."

The firm grip on my face loosens, and he traces his fingers along my jaw before dipping them into the water. Submerging his hand, he lifts his cupped palm full of water back to my face. I flinch and pull back as the water splashes against my face.

"You've made a real mess of yourself." He softly slides his wet hand over my face. Diluted blood—my diluted blood—trickles down his arm as he pulls away. Lifting my burning palms from the water, I find both of my hands completely riddled with scrapes and scratches. Blood still seeping from the deepest of them.

Samuel gently grabs my hand, lightly caressing the back of it with his thumb as he brings it to his face. I tense with resistance, and he squeezes just hard enough to gain my compliance as he pulls my bloody palm to his lips. He places a soft, wet kiss in the center of my palm, leaving his lips stained a deep shade of cherry when he pulls my hand back.

"You're going to let me take care of you, Cora." He presses my hand back into the water before resituating me on his lap. Spreading his thighs, my ass slides between them to the smooth porcelain of the tub. He wraps an arm around me and pulls my back to his chest. The sigh he releases once I'm against him is both eerily comforting and terrifying.

"Plea—" I begin to plead, but I am silenced by a gentle finger over my lips and a shush against my ear.

"You've told me time and time again that you love the ways I take care of you." He pulls a washcloth into the tub and begins sliding it over the sensitive and marred skin of my arm. "You're going to let me, whether you want to or not."

As I sit against him, he continues to clean the mess I made of myself, my heart still pounds as he washes away the blood. Adrenaline, fear, and self-doubt course through my veins as I battle with myself.

Do I run from the monster?

Or submit to the man I've fallen for?

"That's my good girl." Samuel's voice is full of pride when I willingly part my thighs so that he can clean between them. I'm relieved to find his touch isn't sensual, just methodical and caretaker-like as he cleans the last of the blood and cum from me.

Ringing the water from the washcloth, he drapes it over the faucet before wrapping his arms around me and holding me against him. Not tightly or suffocatingly, but lovingly.

"You'll learn," he speaks against the crook of my neck.

"Learn what?" My chin trembles as I ask the question.

"That I know what's best for you and exactly what you need, love." Nearly submerged in now tepid water, goosebumps prickle over my skin at his words.

"Sometimes you might not like what you need," he rubs his hand over the now pimpled flesh of my arm, "but it's always for your best."

My eyelids flutter as I try to keep my welling tears at bay.

How is it possible for my stomach to drop and my heart to swell at the same time?

Is this man going to love me?

And care for me?

Or am I going to wind up like 'the others'?

Dead.

Nothing more than a name—maybe a photo—inside one of Detective Michales' folders.

Samuel pulls the plug, and the sudden gurgle of water draws me from my thoughts. He releases me from his embrace and nudges me slightly, encouraging me to stand. As I do, he rises behind me and climbs from the tub.

Grabbing two towels, he wraps one around me and lifts me out, placing my feet on the plush bathmat before wrapping the other towel around his waist.

Water drips from him as he meticulously dries every inch of my skin. Once he's satisfied, he leads me from the bath and down the hall. We stop outside the room that was mine for a few nights before Samuel had me join him in his bed.

"This will be your room tonight." His words are cold, and I'm surprised to find how much they hurt.

I don't even know if I want to be in his bed, but why doesn't he want me there?

"Why?" I can't seem to stop the question from spilling over my lips.

He opens the door and ushers me inside. His fingers lightly grip my jaw and tilt my chin up toward his face. My breath sputters, and I freeze as he dips his head and presses his lips to mine. Pulling back just a hair, his words vibrate against them. "I think you need a little time to think about what you've done and how to do better."

Releasing my chin and stepping backward, he is quickly on the other side of the threshold.

"I have somewhere to be this evening, and I don't think you're in a state to come." He pauses for a moment as he reaches for the knob. "I trust you'll behave."

The door clicks shut and tears begin to trickle down my face as relief washes over me. Mere seconds of relief... Until my heart is figuratively pulled from my chest.

Running to the door, I grip the handle only to find it doesn't turn. He's locked me in.

"Samuel!" I scream his name as my tender palms painfully slam against the door. But my cries are met with silence.

CHAPTER
TWENTY-SEVEN

SAMUEL

Making my way down the long, tree-shrouded driveway, I head toward the estate for tonight's festivities.

This isn't how I intended to spend tonight.

I had planned to bring Cora with me. We've enjoyed a few girls together, those we've picked up at bars and ones we've hired for a few hours of fun.

I had plans for tonight that we both would have quite enjoyed. My cock twitches at the thought of being deep in her throat as she screams around me from some girl's face being buried between her thighs.

Parking along the circular drive, I park beside two other cars—William's and Edmund's. I make my way up the steps and am pleased to find the help waiting with a freshly poured Sam Adams Utopias. Sipping my beer, I head into the house and toward the study.

As usual, Liz is cozied up on William's lap. The two of them are so engrossed in one another that they barely acknowledge that I have entered the room. Edmund sits at the bar, scrolling through his phone, enjoying a gin and tonic with extra lime.

Grabbing a bar stool, I sit near Edmund. The scraping of my stool along the hardwood floor draws his attention, and without lifting his attention from his phone, he says, "Hey, kid."

Sliding onto the stool, I return his sentiment.

"Watch yourself tonight." He finally lifts his attention to me. "I mean, keep your head down. Grant is still fucking pissed,"

"I got it."

"No one is saying you can't enjoy yourself. Or have a little fun." He stands from his stool and squeezes with shoulder. "Just clean up after yourself."

"No loose ends." I nod as Grant walks into the room with a stunning blonde on his arm. My eyes roam over her tight little body, and I can't help but think how similar her build is to Cora's.

The two of them would be fucking fun together.

Making his way from the bar to where the two of them stand, Edmund makes his play to share in the enjoyment of her this evening. Grant shoots him down quickly, unwilling to let him tarnish an inch of her porcelain skin.

I'm not really feeling tonight's festivities, and knowing Grant's opinion of me at the moment, I don't bother. Even if I wanted her gagging around my cock this evening, Grant would never allow it.

The way Liz saunters over to her, there is no denying her interest—in the blonde or Grant. How quickly she has her tongue down the throat of his little plaything makes it quite apparent how tonight is going to play out.

Fuck...

Watching the two of them, both soft and delicate, yet clawing at each other with a feral need causes my cock to twitch in my pants.

What I would give to watch the two of them.

I rub my palm over my cock, providing some relief as Will pulls Liz from the blonde. "Two million," she pants. "Eddie, love, you get Will's and Grant's too."

"What the fuck, he gets both of them?" The words blurt from me as I continue to rub over my cock—finally ready to play without Cora.

"Maybe when you learn to behave outside this house, we'll treat you a little better, kid," Edmund snarks before leaving the room.

Apparently, he's also taking first dibs on the women down the hall.

Liz's hand rubs beneath her skirt with the same neediness, and I palm my cock. She demands, "Get the fuck out, Samuel."

By the time I make my way to the room Liz uses to hold our entertainment, Edward is already walking out with two blondes and a redhead.

"Sorry, kid," he smirks as he slips his arms around the waists of the blondes. "I'm not a selfish prick. Grab your girl and come join us."

*She's not **my** girl.*

Glancing into the room, I take in the curvaceous brunette waiting patiently on the couch before turning my attention back to Edmund. "Maybe next time." He wastes no time taking his girls down the hall and disappearing into one of the playrooms.

"Up." My tone is flat as I command the brunette. She rises from the couch and begins walking toward me. "Did I fucking tell you to come over here?"

"Sorry." Her eyes fall to the ground. "I thought—"

"You weren't brought here to think." I turn my attention from her to pour myself another drink. "Down the hall, third door on the left. I expect you naked, and on your knees when I get there."

There is a slight hesitation, but her heels begin to click across the room and disappear into the distance.

SAMUEL

Stepping into the room, drink in hand, I am pleased to find the brunette exactly as I commanded. She's removed her dress and the black lingerie that Liz requires of all the girls. Her thighs slightly parted, she's kneeling in the center of the room.

She's much more compliant than I enjoy my women, especially the women I play with here. But she isn't going to be like the others.

Taking a sip of my neat vodka, I walk up to her and slip my finger under her chin. I tip her face up to mine; I stare down at her as I speak. "You're going to follow every command I give you. No questions. No complaints. Understood?"

"Yes." She nods against my hand.

"Good." I release her chin, turn my back to her, and begin opening drawers to find what I need for tonight. "If you want your cunt to be wet, you should get your fingers to work."

She tentatively slides a finger between her thighs, before returning my attention back to the open drawer before me. Pulling out a wand, I close the drawer.

Her fingers work industriously between her legs as I cross the room to her. Light pants and moans fall from her lips as I reach her. Bending down until my face is inches from hers, I drop the wand between her knees.

"Clean your fingers and use it."

Lifting her hands to her mouth, she parts her lips and lays two fingers on her tongue. Circling her lips around them, she moans so incessantly as she sucks that I hold back the urge to roll my eyes at the act she's putting on.

She's nothing like Cora, always enjoying everything I demand of her.

"You don't need to pretend you love the taste of your cunt. I didn't ask if you were enjoying yourself. And if I had any interest in knowing what it tasted like, I'd have your thighs wrapped around my head." I sneer at her. "Now, use the fucking wand like you were told."

She looks like a scolded schoolgirl as she pulls her fingers from her mouth and picks up the wand. Fumbling with it for a minute, she turns it on to the lowest setting and nestles the vibrating head against her cunt.

Her thighs twitch as she settles into the feel of it. Sipping my drink with one hand, I continue to watch her as I use the other to undo my belt buckle. With my belt hanging from the front of my pants, I finish off the last of my vodka before tossing the empty glass onto the bed.

"Turn it up," I demand, gripping the buckle of my belt and pulling it from my pants. She immediately follows my command. Her whimpers grow louder as I loop my belt around her neck and cinch the leather through the buckle before pulling it snugly to her skin.

Holding the wand firmly between her thighs with one hand, she reaches up and swipes over my semi-hard cock through my pants. Her orgasm surprises her, and she grips it firmly as she comes hard from the vibrations of the wand. I tug at the belt, drawing it tighter around her throat, and hiss, "Did I say you could fucking touch me?"

"No." She forces out the word.

"Then remove your fucking hand." I tug again, "And for thinking you can, turn it up higher."

Pulling her hand from me, she clicks the button, and her whole body shakes from the vibrations. Her thighs tremble, and she fights to hold the wand where it belongs.

"Take every orgasm you can from it—" My words are interrupted by the screams of her violent release, her thighs squeezing around the wand as her whole body convulses.

"Higher."

"I can—"

"I didn't ask if you could handle it." I pull the belt a little tighter. "I don't plan on laying a finger on you, but I have a fucking reputation to uphold here. I need to leave you a spent fucking mess."

Swallowing hard, she pushes the button on the wand. She winces at the strength of the highest setting, and my cock throbs at the thought of forcing her to take more. She pulls the wand from her cunt, and I yank the leather in my hand, cinching the belt even tighter until she puts the wand back between her thighs.

Every muscle in her body is tight and shaking violently as she repeatedly tries to scream through the belt that's cutting off her air. Her ass and thighs clench and release as her hips buck wildly against the floor.

"Even now, watching you struggle to breathe as you writhe in blissful agony, you aren't who I want to fuck." I rub my hand over my cock. It's hard.

But not for her...

My eyes might be focused on watching her convulse against the wand I'm forcing her to hold against her cunt, but my mind isn't here. Every thought running through my mind involves slipping into bed with Cora when I get home.

Sliding my cock into her tight, slick cunt.

Relentless strokes of my cock until she's coming undone beneath me.

Fucking her until she's spent, and I'm dripping from her.

"Let me." She trembles the words as her body vibrates harder than the wand on her clit.

"You don't deserve my fucking cock." I drop the belt and leave her trembling on the floor. "You're nothing more than my fucking fluffer tonight."

CORA

"Cora. Love," Samuel's fingers dust along the side of my face as his whispers rouse me from my sleep.

Opening my eyes, I struggle to see in the dark. It takes a moment, but as my eyes adjust all I can make out is his silhouette beside the bed.

"There are things I should have told you." He pulls back the covers and climbs into the bed. He tenderly wraps his arms around me and pulls me against him. Chest to chest, our bare skin touches, and electricity buzzes over my body.

No one makes me feel the way that he does.

Holding me tightly against his hard, muscular body, he presses his lips against mine. They're soft and warm, so inviting that I part mine to let him take more of me. Sweeping his tongue into my mouth, he teasingly rubs it against mine. He doesn't plunder my mouth or roughly claim *it. Instead, he alternates between teasing caresses of his tongue and wet, longing kisses on my lips.*

Samuel's hands roam down my back as he backs away from our kiss. Pulling my leg over his hip, he whispers through our kisses, "I'm sorry I didn't tell you everything about me, love."

His hand rubs up and down the back of my thigh, which is swung over his body, as he kisses me again. The kiss grows deeper, he rolls us until I'm on my back, and he's resting between my thighs.

"I know you must be sore. I'll be gentle, love." He aligns himself with my entrance and takes his time pressing himself into me.

Letting out a moan, I fist the pillow behind my head. My dream is so real and vivid that my heart is racing, and I can barely breathe. The sensations of Samuel on my skin and sliding into me feel so real as I wake up.

"Fuck, I love how you're always so fucking ready to take me." His words vibrate against my neck as he bottoms out inside of me.

This isn't a dream.

"Samuel." My voice cracks as his name trembles from my quivering lips.

"Shhhh." His gentle shush blows against my face before he peppers it with light kisses.

An eerie calmness washes over me as his lips continue to trail down my neck.

I shouldn't like this.

He's a monster.

I should fight him.

"I'd never hurt you like that, love." He lifts his hips and slides back into me to the hilt. His fingers lace around my throat just below my jaw, but he doesn't squeeze. Pressing gently, he stretches my neck to make room for his lips as he works his hips toward a steady pace.

My mind might be unsure, but my body reacts to his touch all the same. Every languid thrust causes me to moan in pleasure, wanting more from him.

"Samu—"

"Do you believe me?" He kisses the words up the side of my neck.

He lifts his head, and our eyes meet. It's dark, but I can see him more than clearly enough. His eyes are warm and full of tenderness. My lips part, but not a sound comes from them.

Because I do...

I do trust him.

"That's what I thought," he whispers. Without breaking our gaze, he slides into me again and again. His eyes boring into mine; every thrust driving deeper than the one before.

Oh God...

It's like he's fucking my soul.

"Sam," I breathlessly whimper his name. Squeezing my legs against his waist, my back arches from the bed as my body explodes beneath him.

"That's it, love." He slides in deeper, burying himself in me before stilling as I continue to quiver around his cock. Dipping his head, he kisses along my neck as he resumes his thrusts. His kisses continue over my collarbone and to the swell of my breasts. Reaching my nipple, he sucks it into his mouth, teasing it aggressively with his tongue and teeth so that I'm unable to control the feral groan rattling from me.

He sucks hard—painfully hard—and releases me with a pop. I'm on the verge of coming when he pulls himself from me and flips me onto my stomach. He reaches beneath me and pulls me onto his lap, slipping back into me as I straddle his thighs.

Kneeling beneath me, he grinds his hips against my ass as his arms snake around my body. His hands sensually roam over my body until one finds my throat, and he whispers in my ear, "Ride my cock until you're coming all over me."

Desperately needing to come after being denied my last orgasm, I slide myself over his length. From this angle, he's so deep that he pleasurably hits my cervix when I take in all of him. Swirling my hips, I continue to slide him in and out of me.

Lightly squeezing around my throat, Samuel pulls my head to his shoulder as I ride him. My groans and whimpers only grow louder when his lips flutter against the side of my neck. He nips at me and sucks my skin into his mouth as he presses my hand between my thighs.

"Make yourself come," he groans into my ear as he rubs my fingers over my clit. Releasing my hand, his travels toward my breast. He rolls and pulls at my nipple, and my senses are on overload.

"Fuck...I'm...going..." I pant the words as my thighs tremble against his. My clit pulses against my fingers, and I clench around him as my orgasm tears through me with a scream.

"To come?" Samuel teasingly whispers before shoving me face-down onto the mattress. He slams into me so hard, I nearly come again.

Fuck, both sides of him feel so good.

Grabbing my throat with enough force to cut off my ability to breathe, he continues to take me hard and fast from behind. I fist the sheets beneath me and whimper through each of his grunt-fueled thrusts.

SAMUEL

"Fuck. You're. Perfect," I growl as I continue to slam into her. She mewls with every relentless drive of my cock, her pulse slowly growing more thready beneath my thumb. Normally, I wouldn't be able to take my eyes from my cock driving into her cunt, but I can't pull my eyes from her tight hold of the sheets. Her grip is so fucking tense it's causing her knuckles to grow more white as she struggles against the urge to fight me for air.

Fuck, she's everything.

Growing more rigid inside of her with every thrust, and knowing I'm done for, I release her throat. Fisting the sheets beside her, my hips spasm against her round ass. My cock twitches, and a breathy groan rattles from my lungs as I fill her with my release, painting her walls with my cum.

Exhausted, I fall against her back. Her skin is flushed, yet cool and covered in sweat, and I can't get enough of how amazing she feels against me. Bracing myself on my forearms, so I don't crush her, I kiss across the salty skin between her shoulders.

"I don't only take care of you," my lips trail up her neck to her ear, "you take care of me, love. More than you'll ever know."

Lifting my hips, I begin to pull my softening cock from her, when she groans, "Stay."

"I'm not going anywhere," I whisper.

"No, stay inside me." Her words are breathy and broken as she pleads with me.

"I'd leave my soul inside you, love."

Holding her hips to keep me buried in her, I roll us both on our sides. She tucks her legs as I bend mine, leaving her spooned tightly against me, my semi-hard cock fully seated inside of her.

My arms wrap securely around her, and I can feel her breaths slowing. As much as I want to talk to her about things, it's late, and I know she's exhausted. And—while the reason for this feeling escapes me—I want to enjoy this moment of the two of us being this connected.

I don't know what it is she's doing to me.

I've never fucked a woman the way we just did. Not once have I ever allowed a woman to use me for their own gratification. I'm the reason they get to come. Or it's the other way round, and I'm taking what I need from them. But I fucking loved the way it felt having her pleasure herself with her fingers and my cock.

And fuck, staring into her eyes.

She truly felt like mine, coming around my cock as I peered into her soul. I feel it even now, with my cock, having grown soft, soaking inside her as she sleeps. Cockwarming when she's awake is controlling, but I don't feel the least bit dominant inside of her right now.

No, this just feels...

Intimate.

***

While my cock has fallen from her, Cora is still in my arms when I wake. Her face is on my chest, and her hair is spayed across my arm and the bed behind her.

She looks like a fucking angel when she sleeps.

"Good morning, love." I place a light kiss on her forehead.

Her eyelids flutter as she tilts her head toward me, and my stomach drops when her eyes meet mine. She pushes back from my embrace and mutters, "This was a mistake."

"Cora." I stretch my arm out toward her as she retreats from the bed.

"I shouldn't have let you..." Her words trail off, and I can tell she's thinking about last night. There is no hiding the shame written on her face.

"Shouldn't have what?" I toss the covers back and climb from the bed. In the event she tries to run, I want to be ready to chase her. I try to hold it back, but my words are fueled with a bit of anger, "Let me fuck you? Ride my cock so hard that your cum trickled down my sac?"

"Samuel." Her voice is pained, and she shakes her head while wrapping the sheet around her body.

"Or maybe it was pleading with me to keep my cock inside of you as you fell asleep in my arms? Which was it, love?" Quickly losing control of my emotions, I can feel my face growing red. My breaths are growing deep and heavy, my nostrils expanding with every heated exhale.

"I can't." Her chin trembles as tears well in her eyes, and she turns her back to me.

"Are my horns fucking showing?" I snap at her. "Do you find me so fucking evil that you can't even look at me in the daylight?"

"You have *fucking* killed women, Samuel." Her voice cracks as she yells, and she spins back to face me. The once-welling tears now stream uncontrollably down her face. Her voice is barely audible when she continues, "You're a murderer."

CORA

"I am. I can't fucking deny who I am or the things that I've done," Samuel nearly shouts at me. His hand slides along his short hair in frustration, and he lets out a heavy sigh as he mutters, "I'm so much fucking worse."

"Worse?" I exclaim.

"I've tried to hide it from you," his eyes dart to the scrapes and bruises from yesterday, "but I couldn't. You've seen it with your face pressed against the cobblestones."

"I...I don't understand."

"You aren't the first woman I've fucked with their face buried in the ground." His tone is flat as he explains, "I don't even know how many of them there have been over the years."

My stomach drops, and I'm filled with nausea. "Why?"

"They don't matter." He paces and his voice is on the verge of sounding frantic. "I'm trying so fucking hard, Cora."

"Trying to do what?"

"To keep these uncontrollable urges at bay." He rounds the bed and takes a step toward me. I quickly realize that I have nowhere to go but backward. I recoil with every step he takes until I find myself in the corner.

His hands slam into the wall, flanking my face, and boxing me in as he braces his weight on his forearms. My heart pounds, and I can barely breathe as he looms over me. Looking up at him, our eyes meet. While his face is riddled with anger—pure fucking rage—all I can see is the softness of his eyes. And I can't bring myself to look away.

"You weren't the first of them, Cora." He shakes his head as he presses his forehead to mine.

"What are you saying, Samuel?" I struggle through my tears to push the words out.

"I've never fought it before. I've given in to every fucking urge and need." His words are slow and heavy, his warm breath blowing over my face with every word.

"The last time?" I ask, completely unsure if I want to know the answer.

"Chicago."

"You fucking raped a woman in Chicago, then flew home early to—"

"I didn't fuck anyone in Chicago," he gruffly interrupts me. "I followed her. I grabbed her with every intention of fucking her. Wanting nothing more than to hear her screaming and gasping for air as I took what I needed from her."

"Sam..." I almost sob his name as my eyes fall to the floor. So overwhelmed by his confessions, I don't know how to react.

"I couldn't fucking do it." He slips a finger under my chin and tips my face back up toward his. "I couldn't even fucking get hard for her. Even when I'm weak, my cock knows you're fucking it for me."

"Because you couldn't get it up," I scoff. "I'm supposed to feel better?"

"The party last night. The one you were supposed to come to with me. I spent two million on a whore there last night." He firmly grips my chin when I try to look away again, "I didn't lay a fucking finger on her. My cock never fucking left my pants. I had no interest in fucking her. The entire fucking time I fantasized about coming home to you. About coming home and fucking you."

His grip tightens on my chin, the force of his grip hovering on the edge of being painful. He lowers his face until there is just a breath of space between us.

"You, Cora." He leans against me and exhales, "Just fucking you."

His lips press firmly against mine, and the undeniable electricity between the two of us shoots through my body. Flooding every nerve, it momentarily washes away every feeling of betrayal and disgust.

"You're all I fucking want." He speaks against my lips, and his voice is suddenly laced with anguish. "You make me fucking better, love. I can't fucking let you go."

"Sam." His name vibrates from my lips to his.

"I'll give you a little space," he releases my chin and takes a step back from me, "but you're not fucking leaving."

Samuel walks from the room, and my body slides down the wall until I'm sitting on the floor with my knees pulled to my chest. Dropping my face between my knees, I sob uncontrollably. My tears dampen the sheet as they continue to fall from my face.

How is it possible to care this much for a fucking monster?

To fucking...love him?

CHAPTER
THIRTY-TWO

SAMUEL

Cora's sobs follow me as I make my way down the hall to my bedroom. The one I used to share with her.

The place she belongs.

Where she will be when all this is over.

As messy as this fucking is, I meant every damn word. I want to be better for her. I want to deserve her. She will be the last for me.

*She **will** be staying.*

As much as I want to trust that she won't run, I grab my tablet from the nightstand and pull up the alarm system. Swiping over the options, I turn on all the sensors. She won't be able to crack a window without every house within a mile radius knowing that she has triggered the alarm.

Stepping into the bathroom, I turn on the shower and step in before the water warms. The icy water is shockingly cold. So cold it burns my goose-pimpled skin. I hiss through the discomfort as it slowly warms to a scaling hot temperature.

I love the smell of Cora on my skin, but I need to think. With my palms pressed to the shower wall, the hot beads rain over my head and down my body. Water blows from my face with every soothing breath that exhales from my lungs. It's relaxing and exactly what I need to figure out how to fix things between us.

I know what I need to do.

Turning off the water, I grab the towel from the hook and wrap it around my waist without bothering to dry the rest of me. Walking across my room, water continues to drip down my body, leaving wet footprints in my wake.

Heading into my closet, I quickly dry off and pull on a pair of dress pants and a pressed white shirt. After putting on my shoes, I work on my cufflinks as I begin walking toward Cora's room.

The doorbell rings, drawing my attention away from my original destination. It rings again, and from the corner of my eye, I notice Cora, eyes red and still cocooned in a sheet, stepping from her room. We make our way down the stairs as it continues to chime over and over again. It is either stuck, or someone on the other side is quite intent on getting our attention.

"Jesus fucking Christ!" I shout. "I'm coming."

Opening the door, I'm caught off-guard by our unexpected guest.

"Mr. Millington," Detective Michales greets me. "I was hoping to get a few minutes of your time."

Cora steps past the threshold and quickly garners his attention. "Ms. Durant, pleased to see you're still alive."

She turns toward him, exposing the cut on her face from the driveway. His hand slams against the door, and he begins to press himself inside. "Did he do that to you? Did he hit you?"

"I don't recall inviting you inside," I shove my body in front of him to prevent him from making it over the threshold. "And as I've said before, if you want to talk to me or Cora, it will be through my attorney."

As though he didn't hear a word I just said, he continues to push his way through the door as he asks Cora, "Do you need help?"

While it's only a mere second, it feels like minutes of deafening silence when she hesitates to answer him. Minutes in which a life in prison flashes before my eyes.

"No." She shakes her head. Lifting her hands to expose her well-scratched palms, she continues, "I fell in the driveway. Stupid cobblestones weren't designed for stilettos."

"Happy?" I snark while pushing the door shut, forcing him to take a step backward. "You know my attorney's number; try using it."

Closing the door, I immediately turn to face Cora. I stare at her for a moment, slightly surprised that after our interaction this morning, she didn't take the out Michales offered her. Before I can say a word, she blurts out, "This doesn't mean we're okay."

Maybe not.

But it means more than you realize.

We stand in the foyer in silence, minutes passing as both of us are at a loss for words.

The bell rings again, in quick succession from the finger laying on it from the other side of the door. Flinging open the door without diverting my attention from Cora, I shout, "For fuck's sake. Do you not fucking understand what call my attorney means?"

"Sorry," a deep voice bellows, and I turn to find a man I've never met standing on my front step. He's a huge man—several inches taller than me and easily carrying fifty additional pounds of muscle—the kind of guy I didn't exactly enjoy going head-to-head with on the field. If he weren't intimidating, the fact that he has a blond clone standing behind him definitely would make up for it.

"We don't exactly deal with lawyers," the blond clone chuckles from the back.

Removing his sunglasses, the man on the threshold presses the door lightly while exposing the gun tucked into his waistband. "Are you going to invite us in?"

"Probably not." I push against the door. "I don't fucking know you."

"No. You don't." He puts his full weight into the door and shoves his way inside forcefully. "But you know our boss, and you've kept something you shouldn't have."

CHAPTER
THIRTY-THREE

CORA

The front door flings open, and Samuel stumbles backward into the foyer. Two massive walls of men walk through the now-empty doorway.

"The boss has a few things to discuss with you, too, Cora." A tall, dark-haired man comprised of nothing but muscles stalks toward me. "You don't get to just walk away from the life she's provided you with."

His enormous paw wraps around my arm, and I wince in pain as squeezes me. He yanks me into his side, and I slam against him with a thud.

"Get your fucking hands off her." Samuel shoves the man holding me, quickly pulling me into his arms when the huge paw releases its grip. "She's not fucking going anywhere."

"The boss wants her back," the dark-haired man snarls.

Wrapping his arms tighter around me as though they are a shield, Samuel rebuts, "And I told your boss I'd pay. Whatever she fucking wants. Cora's done with that life."

I swallow hard at his words, having no idea the lengths that Samuel is willing to go to keep me.

"I work for her." I vehemently shake my head, "She doesn't fucking own me."

Both the men laugh at my apparent naivety. I've told myself for years I could stop whenever I wanted, but anytime I tried, she always dangled one more job before me. One that was always too fucking good to walk away from.

One like Samuel's.

So focused on the man before us, neither of us realize that the other has made his way behind us until he's pressing the muzzle of a gun to Samuel's temple. His voice is dark and terrifying as he says, "If you want us to go easy on her, and you don't want to watch her bleed, you're going to let go."

Samuel reluctantly loosens his embrace, and the dark-haired man wastes no time pulling me against him. His free hand pulls at the sheet covering me as his fingers roam down my body.

"Don't you fucking touch her," Samuel growls as the blond with the gun wraps an arm around his throat and presses the muzzle painfully hard against his temple. It digs into his skin, and his face contorts in pain from the pressure.

"Just curious if she has a golden fucking cunt under here. Is that it, sweetheart?" the dark-haired man snickers as his hand finds my bare pussy. "The amount of money the boss turned down to get her back. It must be fucking magical."

Futilely, I fight against his hold, but he only squeezes his thick arm tighter around me as he presses his finger into me. Pulling it from me and bringing it back to his face, he pauses to look at the wetness on his finger before sucking it into his mouth. "Tastes like any other whore's cunt if you ask me."

"You Motherfucker." Samuel fights against the man holding him. Rage is coursing through his body. His nostrils flare, and I see the darkness in his eyes that chills me to my core. "I'll **fucking** kill you."

The dark-haired man pulls the sheet from me and lets it fall to the floor, leaving me naked before all of them. I can feel the boss' men's eyes hungrily roaming over my body, but Samuel's stay locked on my face.

"If you didn't like that," I can feel the dark-haired man undoing his pants behind me as he speaks, and I know what's coming. "You're going to fucking hate watching me see if it's her ass that's so fucking special."

Tears stream down my face, and I scream as he shoves me against the entryway table. The rough edge of the marble agonizingly juts into my hips as he forcefully bends me over the narrow table until my face hits the wall. I fight against him, but he's too fucking strong.

Feeling him press between my ass, I see Samuel jerk violently from the corner of my eye. His head snaps back, and the gut-churning sound of a bone breaking fills the room. Blood pours from the blond man.

"You son of a bitch." He whacks Samuel against the side of his head with the gun. "You fucking broke my nose."

It draws the dark-haired man's attention enough that he stops trying to shove himself into my ass. Instead, he pulls me back and slams my face into the marble with such force that it cracks. Blood flows down my face, the force of the fall reopening cut on my cheek.

Done with me—at least for now—the dark-haired man puts away his cock and lets me fall to the floor. I crumple against the hardwood floor, and everything is hazy as he storms toward Samuel.

"She's a fucking whore." The dark-haired man pulls a switchblade from his pocket and flips it open. "You should've just given her back."

Without hesitation, he lifts his arm and thrusts the knife into Samuel's chest. He grunts, and crimson immediately spreads across the white shirt.

"Samuel!" I scream his name as his eyes go wide from the pain of the knife being pulled from his chest.

"Shut that bitch up!" the dark-haired man shouts before shoving the knife into Samuel's gut. The darkness in his eyes dims as he falls to the floor a few feet from me. Blood pools around his body as he stares at me.

"I'm sorry," he mutters as his lids flutter, and his eyes fall shut.

"No!" I wail as the blond lifts his foot, everything going black the moment it hits my face.

SAMUEL

Fighting to open my eyes, I groan in my pain. My body feels like it was used as a fucking punching bag. Carefully, I shift my weight; my hand slips across the slick hardwood as I try to push myself from the floor.

Blood.

So much fucking blood.

Cora!

"Cora!" I call her name when I realize she's no longer lying on the floor beside me.

Struggling to look around, I no longer see the two men that burst into my home. I somehow force myself onto my hands and knees through the searing pain, and I crawl toward the open front door. Any evidence of my visitors or Cora is long gone.

As I grab at the door frame, my bloodied hands slide along the wood as I try to bring myself to my feet. Unsteady and using the wall for support, I grab my keys from the bowl on the now-cracked marble table by the door.

I need help...

Stumbling down the steps, coppery smelling droplets fall from me as I cross the cobblestone driveway to my car. Climbing into the driver's seat, I head to the only person I know who will be able to find her.

Battling to keep my eyes open during the short drive, I'm relieved when I make it to the gate. Even more so when I find it open, allowing me to drive up to the house without the option of being turned away.

I pull to a stop in the driveway and climb from the blood-stained leather. Standing with a breathy grunt, I continue to take short, shallow breaths as I force myself up the front steps and onto the porch.

My arm trembles from the throbbing pain in my shoulder, causing my hand to shake as I press the button for the doorbell. Watching it shake, I realize that it's covered in blood. Both of my hands are absolutely covered in the stuff.

It's practically pouring from my body, flowing down my arms, trickling from my fingers, and soaking my clothes.

Answer the fucking door...

...before I'm dead on your front step.

Pressing it again, I hold it with the same audacity that Michales rang mine earlier today.

"I'm coming," Abigail calls from the other side of the door. The door opens, and her eyes immediately widen upon the sight of me. She swallows hard and takes a small step back, looking as though she desperately needs to put distance between the two of us.

"Aren't you going to invite me in?" I push out the words through the searing pain in my chest. Taking advantage of the small space she left on the threshold, I nudge her out of the way as I help myself into their home.

"Grant!" Her voice trembles with fear as she calls for him.

It takes only a second for him to react to her desperate call for him, and he joins us in the foyer almost instantly. With how protective he is of her, I'm surprised he didn't come barreling into the hall to protect her from me. He pauses briefly when he sees me—*I knew this was the last place I should have come*—and I can easily read the disdain on his face.

He quickly positions himself between me and Abigail. Stepping toward him, I extend my bloody hand for a truce—or maybe support for my wavering body—and mumble, "I fucked up..."

"What the fuck are you doing here." Grant scowls, ignoring my outstretched hand.

Grabbing my side, and struggling to stay on my feet, I take a shallow breath before answering him. "I know you fucking hate me, but I need your help."

"I told you, kid," he shakes his head, "I'm not cleaning up your messes anymore. You're on your own."

"It's not..." The burning ache in my side is nearly unbearable, and I press my hand against the wound. Grunting at the self-inflicted pressure, blood oozes between my fingers. "They took her."

"Took who?" Abigail steps around Grants as she questions me.

"Cora," I struggle to answer as I fumble to pull my phone from my pocket. Offering it to Grant, I force out the words as my vision begins to blacken around the edges. "I need you to find her."

Looking at Grant for a moment, Abigail hesitantly takes the phone from me. My bloody hands stain her porcelain skin as she slides it from my fingers.

"Please," I cough out as my legs give way beneath me, and everything goes black.

CORA

Coming to, my face is fucking killing me. Actually, my whole fucking head is killing me. I try to open my eyes, but it almost feels like one of them is glued shut.

You did get kicked in the fucking face, Cora.

Barely able to open the other, I struggle to see as I lean into the muscular chest I'm resting against. Running my fingers over the dress shirt, I whisper, "Samuel."

His hand comfortingly rubs up and down my back, while lightly pulling me tighter to him. Carefully sweeping the hair from my tender face, he takes his time tucking it behind my ear as he whispers, "No, sweetheart."

I startle at the voice—immediately placing it as the dark-haired man from the house—and he wraps his huge hands around me to keep me from moving. Both of his hands are on my skin, meaning I'm still completely bare as I sit on his lap. My only comfort comes from the fact that he's still fully dressed beneath me, and none of him is inside of me.

"Where is Samuel?" I struggle to ask, both for fear of the answer and the throbbing pain echoing through my skull that accompanies every syllable.

"Your boyfriend?" the blond scoffs from the driver's seat of the car. "I don't think you'll need to worry about him anymore. I'd be surprised if he didn't bleed out before we got your limp body in the car."

Fighting back the urge to scream in agony, tears silently roll down my cheeks. The salty droplets burn as they roll over the open wound on my cheek, but the pain they cause is nothing like the heavy feeling in my heart.

Samuel...

"Speaking of blood," the deep voice of the dark-haired man beneath me demands my attention, "you've ruined my suit, and I'm going to expect you to pay for that."

"Do you take check or card?" My voice oozes with insolence and sarcasm.

"Neither." He fists the hair at the back of my head so hard my scalp burns, the pain radiating around my head so violently that stars flutter across my vision. Yanking my head back and forcing me to look at him, a wicked smile spreads across his face as he says, "This establishment only takes pussy and ass."

"Are you seriously going to fuck her while I drive us down the highway?" the blond questions. "It's bad enough she's fucking naked on your lap in broad daylight."

A devilishly dark laugh vibrates against me from the man holding me tightly to him.

"I'll wait," His hands roam over my body, and a sickening feeling grows in my stomach at his touch. "We're only a few minutes from the boss's place."

"Enough time to do it twice, I'm guessing," I quip, and I can't help but smirk when the driver doesn't hide his laughter.

I've dealt with enough men like him to know how they function. Turned on or angry. The muscle-clad asshole isn't capable of dealing with both feelings at the same time. And in the end, one is going to be much easier for me to endure.

At least in the long run.

His huge, meaty paw of a hand slaps my cheek so hard that the sound reverberates around the car. It's not enough for him, and he hits me again before gripping my face with enough force to bruise my cheeks and jaw.

"You're a real mouthy fucking bitch." His spittle lands on my face as the angered words spew from his mouth.

"So, I've been told," I shrug. "Your mom probably should've been a little mouthier, if you know what I mean."

The blond laughs uncontrollably.

Who doesn't love a well-timed, 'your mom should've swallowed,' joke?

Apparently, the butt of the joke.

Throwing me forward, he slams my face against the dashboard with such force that I almost black out. He shoves my near-limp body to the floor between his feet and begins undoing his pants.

"Let's see how much shit you talk when you have my cock shoved in your mouth." He fumbles with his zipper as we pull to a stop.

"You can't afford to put your cock in her, Adam," a familiar woman's voice shouts from the elevator bank beside the car. "Unless you plan on working for free, I suggest you tuck that back into your pants."

I release a heavy sigh of relief as he zips back up. Pulling me back into his lap, he whispers, "She won't always be around. I intend to take my payment."

CHAPTER
THIRTY-SIX

GRANT

"Samuel," I lightly slap my palm against his face, trying to stir him. Feeling along his neck, I struggle to find a pulse. When I finally do, it's so light and thready that I nearly miss it.

The sound of Abigail pressing buttons on her phone draws my attention. "Don't."

"We need to call for help," she protests as she stares down at his lifeless body and the pool of blood I'm kneeling in.

"There'll be too many fucking questions if they come here. Michales is going to have a fucking field day."

Pulling at his arms, I drag his listless body to a seated position. "Help me get him up and to the car, kitten."

We both pull an arm over our shoulders and practically drag him to the front door. Stepping over the threshold, thunder cracks across the sky, and a light rain begins to fall.

The fucking luck.

As I hold the brunt of his weight, Abigail opens the passenger door to my Maserati parked out front, and we slide him into the car.

"You are so buying new seats, kid," I grumble as I lean over him to secure the seatbelt. As I stand, Abigail is opening the rear door. "I need you to stay here, kitten."

"Sir?"

"I need you to clean up his car and the foyer." I cup her face. "Remove any trace of this happening here. Call one of the guys to come help you and send another to his place in case there's a mess there."

She nods her head in agreement.

Always so willing to follow my commands.

"I wasn't here. I left this morning, and you don't know what's happened. Understood?"

"Yes, Sir," she replies as I place a quick kiss on her lips—*hopefully not my last*—before climbing into the car. The engine purrs as I turn on the ignition, leaving Abigail standing alone in my taillights as I peel down the driveway.

Rain pours from the sky, making it difficult to see as I race toward the hospital before Samuel bleeds out in my car. His chin lolls against his chest, as I continue to take turns at unsafe speeds—especially in this weather.

Pulling into the hospital's emergency bay, I flash my lights and honk my horn to get the attention of the staff inside. Climbing from the car, I frantically yell for help.

This shit needs to be believable.

"My friend...we were attacked...help him."

Samuel is drenched in blood as they pull him from my car and lay him on the stretcher. Rain falls over his body, leaving a bloody river swirling against the asphalt beneath the gurney as they rush him inside.

"Sir?" A nurse taps my shoulder and gestures to the blood covering my shirt. "Are you okay?"

"It...It's not mine." I look down and feign surprise. "I'm fine. Just help him."

"He's in good hands," she reassures me. "Let's get you inside and make sure you're okay."

She ushers me down the hall to a private exam room before asking, "Is there anyone you need us to call? Let them know you're here?"

"Abigail. I was supposed to be home soon."

"Of course. Give me her number, and I'll get someone to call her to let her know where you are. And for your friend?"

"His girlfriend, Cora, is out of town, and I don't have her number." I pause for a moment. "Can you please ask Abigail to get in touch with her?"

A doctor joins us in the room and goes through the full gambit of examinations to ensure that I wasn't harmed in the attack that left Samuel near death.

"And my friend?" I call to the doctor before he leaves the room.

"They've rushed him up to surgery." He turns back to face me with a solemn look on his face. "He has two quite serious stab wounds, and quite frankly, it's a miracle he made it to the hospital. If you're a god-fearing man, I would say that now is the time to pray."

I merely nod my understanding.

I know the lengths I would go to if someone were to take Abigail.

If he came to me for help, instead of the hospital, as blood gushed from his body, she must be really fucking important to him.

"I'm going to leave you some scrubs." The nurse pats the folded gray clothes on the bed beside me. "I don't want you to have to sit in your bloody and wet clothes as you wait for your friend."

"Thank you." I stand and peel off my soaked shirt.

"And we've called your wife. She's on her way," the nurse informs me before leaving me in privacy to change.

My wife...

DETECTIVE MICHALES

Grant Geyer and Samuel Millington's names coming over the police scanner was like getting the perfect present on Christmas morning. I may be on administrative leave, but knowing the precinct is going to send two incompetent patrolmen to take a statement, nothing could stop me from heading over there.

Flipping on my car's sirens, I waste no time crossing town and pulling into the emergency bay. When I climb from the car, I immediately recognize the expensive car parked beside me. Pressing my face to the glass to peer through the window, I take note of the blood-soaked passenger seat.

"Detective Michales." I flash my badge at entry. "I'm here for the mugging—Mr. Geyer and Mr. Millington."

I don't for a second believe that this was a mugging.

The woman at the desk types on her keyboard and informs me, "Mr. Millington is still in surgery. I believe Mr. Geyer is in the waiting room."

"Thank you." I begin walking from the desk as I speak.

Seeing Mr. Geyer, I head straight over to him and take a seat beside him. Keeping my voice low, I ask, "What happened? Did one of them finally fight back?"

"I don't know what you're talking about." He shakes his head, denying my accusation. "We were leaving The Jellyfish after an early lunch to discuss some business matters, and a guy attacked us in the parking lot."

"He's in surgery, and you're sitting here completely unscathed?"

"The kid." He shakes his head. "He's fucking stupid sometimes. He put up a fight when the guy demanded his wallet. And then, it all just happened so fast."

"And you brought him here? Instead of calling for an ambulance?"

"I didn't think. I jus—"

"Grant." His words are cut short when a gorgeous blonde comes running into the waiting room. He stands from his seat, and she practically jumps into his arms. "Thank God you're okay."

"I'm fine." His hands slide along her face, cupping it as he leans down to kiss her.

"And Sam?" she asks the moment he pulls back. Mr. Geyer shakes his head, and she gasps, "Is he?"

"He's in surgery, kitten," he consoles her. "Did you get in touch with Cora?"

"I left a message, but—"

"I'm going to need to get her number from you." I interject myself into their conversation.

"Sure." She reaches in her pocket for her phone. "I must've left it at home in my rush to get here."

"I have your card at home. Plenty of them." Mr. Geyer's eyes dart toward me. "We'll get it to you after we make sure our friend is okay. Now, if you'll excuse us."

Taking his less-than-subtle hint, I stand from the uncomfortable waiting room chair and head toward the exit. I am apparently leaving in the nick of time as I pass the two patrol officers at the exit.

Making a beeline to my car, I flip open my notebook the moment I'm behind the wheel, quickly jotting down every detail of Mr. Geyer's recount of the alleged events and the conversation I overheard between him and the blonde.

Finishing the details, I leave myself a few notes:

Mid-Day Mugging
—Fucking Bullshit!

It's all too perfect.
Where is Cora Durant?
DEAD???

Closing the notebook, I toss it onto the passenger seat before pulling out my phone.

You available?

HARPER
At work.

Don't lie to me Harper.

I'm not.

You can call them.

I don't get off until eleven.

I'll be there at midnight.

Just you.

Ok.

Time to see if Edmund's little slut has more use than just sucking my cock.

CORA

"Feeling a little better?" The raspy female voice startles me from the doorway, and I attempt to cover myself.

"Darling," she scoffs, "You don't have anything I haven't seen a thousand times before. And we all watched you walk naked through the front door an hour ago."

Grabbing a little first aid kit and a washcloth, she takes a seat on a small wooden stool beside the tub that I'm soaking in.

"Thank you." I gesture at the tub. "For this."

"You looked like it was needed." She dips the washcloth into the water and wrings the excess from it. The drops and suds splatter over the sleeves of her silk shirt, leaving sputters of darkened fabric and likely ruining it.

Lifting the cloth to my face, she gently cleans around the cuts on my cheeks and my unbelievably tender, swollen eye. She's meticulous and careful, and I can't help but think about Samuel bathing me. How loving and intimate it was as he slid the cloth over my skin.

I take a deep breath, but it does nothing to stop the tears from trickling down my face.

They killed him.

And it's my fault.

He's dead because of me.

"Oh, Darling." She blows over my cheek, drying the skin to place a butterfly bandage. "You broke the rules. You don't fall for the John."

Bringing the bandage to my face, she squeezes together the open cut on my cheek, and I flinch when her well-manicured nails dig into my skin.

"And you never cross your Madame." She continues to squeeze the tender skin unnecessarily hard as she places a second bandage.

"I'm sorry, Madame," I grit the words through my pain, and she releases my face.

"Sorry doesn't make the other girls forget about your betrayal. You need to be punished." She dips her hands in the water to rinse my blood from them. Shaking them as she stands, she grabs a towel to try them. "You will need to serve as a lesson to the others what happens when you leave me."

"I didn't—"

"You've been playing house with him for weeks on my dime." She looms over the tub. "And look at you, so fucking battered and bruised that I couldn't sell you for twenty dollars to start paying it off."

"What are you going to do to me?"

"I haven't quite decided yet, Darling." Her heels click across the floor as she brings me a towel. She holds it open, silently instructing me to get out of the tub. As I stand, she wraps it around me, the bottom dusting against the water and soaking the edges.

"I'm not going to kill you." She takes my hand and helps me to step over the high edge of the clawfoot tub. "I need you to be a constant memorable reminder, not a quickly forgotten scare. I'll have one of the girls bring you some ice for that eye."

"Madame?" I call after her in vain as she walks from the bathroom.

Not bothering to find any clothes, I climb into the bed with the towel still wrapped around me. Grabbing the pillow, I wrap my arms around it and squeeze it tightly. I bury my face in it to hide my screams. Violently expelling my lungs into the pillow until I'm exhausted, I continue to hold it to my face to muffle my uncontrollable sobs.

I try to get some rest while I'm left alone, but when I close my eyes, all I can see is Samuel.

The knife sliding from his stomach. Him crumpling to the floor. A pool of blood oozing from beneath him as he stared into my eyes. Those normally dark eyes filled with sadness and regret like nothing I have ever seen.

Silently telling me how sorry he was as he slipped away.

SAMUEL

"Fuck," I groan as I groggily wake up. The pain in my side is now a throbbing ache instead of a searing pain. My eyelids flutter, but they feel ungodly heavy and as though I have no control over them—as with the rest of my body.

There are people here—wherever this is—but I can't keep my eyes open long enough to see who they are. I can hear them talking, but my head's so fuzzy that I can't place any of their voices.

How fucking high am I?

"Relax, kid." a deep voice echoes through my head. "You're lucky to be alive."

Fragments of a thousand thoughts run through my clouded mind, but darkness begins to creep back over me before I can put them together.

***

Opening my eyes, I look around, trying to place my surroundings. Slowly, I turn my head, and I'm surprised at who I find sitting beside my bed.

"Grant?" His name cracks from the dry and scratchiness of my throat.

"Welcome back, kid." His voice has a hint of warmth to it that I'm not used to. At least not when he's talking to me. He presses the call button resting on the bed and alerts the nurses' station that I'm awake.

"Cora?" I ask, but Grant doesn't have a chance to answer before the doctor enters the room.

"We can get into that when he's done checking you over," Grant reassures me as he stands from the bedside seat and leaves the room.

"You gave us all quite a scare, Mr. Millington." The doctor flashes a—*too bright*—flashlight into my eyes as he talks. "You'd lost a lot of blood by the time you got here. We were a little worried for the first couple of days."

"Days?" I fight the overwhelming urge to climb from this bed and run after Cora, even though I can barely lift my own head from the thin mattress beneath me.

The doctor continues his examination, thoroughly checking my vitals and examining the cleanly sutured stab wounds in my shoulder and abdomen.

"These are healing nicely." He replaces the gauze covering my stomach before taking a seat beside my bed. "But I'll be honest, I'm a little more concerned with what we found from the laceration on your scalp."

"I got whacked in the head, Doc." I lightly shake my head. "I've taken plenty of helmets to the head over the years. It'll be fine."

"That was actually the issue, Mr. Millington. We did a head CT to ensure there weren't any contusions or brain bleeds from where your friend said you hit your head on the parking lot." He pauses briefly to open my chart on the tablet in his lap. "It showed something concerning, so we ran additional tests. The PET scan showed significant evidence of Traumatic Brain Injury."

"I don't quite understand what you're saying."

"It's likely that years of helmet-to-helmet contact is the culprit. I would assume that you've played since childhood to have been as successful at it as you were."

"Yes." I nod. "Since about ten."

"There isn't much we can do in terms of treatment, other than behavioral therapies. But if you're suffering from things such as a lack of impulse control, fits of anger, lack of restraint, or irritability, this would very likely be the cause. And treatment would help."

"I don't," I cross my arms over my chest, knowing it's a lie, "have any of those issues."

"Well, you're quite lucky then." He continues to go over the other symptoms for a few minutes before leaving me.

Grant, who was waiting just outside the door, reenters as he leaves.

"Cora." I wince through her name as I struggle to sit myself up in the bed.

Grant shakes his head. "I went through the phone you gave to Abigail. She's not at her home address. I tried to trace her phone from the number in your contacts, but it's off. And unfortunately, with our phones scrubbing content every twelve hours, without more information from you, I really didn't have much to go on."

"I need to find her." I swing my feet off the hospital bed, and I groan through the shooting pain in my side as I push myself to my feet. My legs wobble beneath me, and Grant catches me before I fall to the floor.

"Get your ass back in the bed, kid," he demands in a fatherly tone. "There is absolutely nothing that you can do to find her that I can't help you do from this hospital room. "Abigail is bringing my laptop. We'll find her."

We have to.

I don't know what I'd do without her.

CHAPTER
FORTY

CORA

Madame is a cruel fucking woman. She's allowed me
free roam of her home since the men brought me here,
but she uses every opportunity she has to remind me
how great I have it, and that my punishment for
betraying her is coming.

My mind has literally been running wild with the things
she can or might do to me.

Letting one of her goons beat me beyond recognition.

*Killing me—even if she has repeatedly told me that's not an
option.*

Selling me off.

*She has a few international clients that would make Samuel
look like a fucking teddy bear. Years of abuse and body muti-
lation make death seem like the better option.*

Or maybe she'll just let Adam loose.

He's dying to make good on his threats from the car.

Sitting at the counter and sipping my coffee, I can feel him entering the room. It's as if the air literally grows cold in his presence, making the feel of his eyes burning into my skin that much more noticeable. Goosebumps prickle over my skin as he approaches, not stopping until I can feel him pressed to my back. My heart pounds in my chest, and I try desperately to maintain my steady breathing.

I don't want him to know that I'm afraid.

His knuckles drag down the back of my bare neck, and a chill runs down my spine as he whispers, "Alone at last, my mouthy little bitch."

"Hey," the blond man who brought me here shakes his head from the entry at the other side of the large kitchen, "you know the boss has said she's off-limits."

"And she won't fucking know if you don't fucking tell her," he barks as his hand begins sliding down the front of my loose tank top. "I'll even hold her down to give you a chance to get your dick wet. Or you could fucking leave and mind your own fucking business."

The blond pulls out a stool and defiantly takes a seat at the other side of the counter. I silently mouth the words, "thank you," as Adam leans closer.

"Lock your doors at night, little bitch, because I will get you alone. And I **will** get what I want from you. What you fucking owe me," he grits the words against my ear before pulling up a stool beside the blond. Leaning into him, he seethes, "And you're going to fucking get what you deserve, too."

Turning his attention back to me, Adam's eyes roam over my body as he repeatedly slips his switchblade open and closed. Occasionally, he pauses to roll the open blade through his fingers and lick his lips before continually taunting me with the blade.

As much as I don't want to sit here and allow him to continue to emotionally torment me, it's safer than winding up anywhere with him alone.

"Good. You're all here," Madame chirps as she joins us in the kitchen. The heavy thud of a book hitting the countertop startles me, and I jump in my seat. She slides the book toward me. "I've heard you enjoy reading. Do you know this one?"

The Scarlet Letter

Before I have a moment to react, Adam grabs my wrists. Madame lifts my coffee mug from between my arms as I try to pull them from Adam's tight hold. Pouring my remaining coffee down the drain, she addresses me with an inflection more suitable for a coffee date than torture. "You've been my best girl for years, Cora. I'm going easy on you. Remember that if you think about crossing me again."

Adam yanks my hands hard, forcing me to stand as he pulls my chest over the cold granite. He stands, and the blond takes my wrists from him, holding me equally as tightly. Placing a bottle of vodka down on her way out of the kitchen, Madame instructs them, "Clean it when you're finished."

Rounding the island, Adam presses himself firmly against my ass as he leans his chest against my back. He flicks open the switchblade in front of my face, then uses it to cut the straps of my tank top and bra. Yanking them both from my skin, he grinds his cock against my ass and whispers in my ear, "You have no idea how much I'm going to fucking enjoy this."

He drags the tip of the blade along my skin with a light feathery touch, and I shout, "Just fucking do it!"

"Foreplay, little bitch," he snickers against my skin as he continues to grind his hips against me. "Foreplay."

He shoves his forearm against my upper back and uses his weight to pin me to the counter as he takes his time pressing the knife tip through my skin. Gritting my teeth, I fist my hands so hard that my nails dig into my skin as I try to manage the pain.

"One way or another," he sloppily kisses against the back of my ear as I squirm beneath him, "You're going to fucking scream for me today."

The knife slowly cuts through my skin, and I scream as he carves through my flesh over and over again. Blood trickles over my shoulder and begins pooling under my cheek as I cry out in agony with every movement of his hand. My legs are trembling beneath me when he drops the bloody blade on the counter.

Twisting open the bottle beside him, he takes a swig before pouring it over my back. I shriek as the alcohol hits the open wounds. Slamming the bottle back on the counter, he licks through the bloodied vodka on my back.

His disgusting tongue drags along my skin, up my neck to my ear before he whispers, "That was fucking great for me. How was it for you?"

DETECTIVE MICHALES

Anything?

HARPER
I told you, I'd let you know.

I feel like you aren't even trying, Harper.

If you really want your family to know how you're paying for college, I'm fine it that.

I'll see him tonight.

I will try to get something.

Try hard.

I know first hand how persuasive that mouth of yours can be.

Despite a perfect little body, a tight fucking pussy, and quite a talented mouth, she's been proving otherwise useless. At least in terms of my investigation. Forcing her to engage in Edmund Parker's depravities, which I don't think she disapproves of nearly as much as she complains about, I was expecting more. Apparently, I overestimated things, because getting her ass pounded red doesn't come with pillow talk.

Or maybe she's playing both sides.

Since she's fucking useless, and I didn't find a shred of evidence to corroborate their story at The Jellyfish, I'm going to take advantage of the fact that everyone is at the hospital watching over Mr. Millington.

Parked about a mile away, I climb the stone wall that surrounds the majority of his property and begin the couple of acres walk to reach his estate.

No time like the present to look around.

This time, I plan to make it well past the front door.

Reaching the main entrance, I pull the lock pick set from my back pocket. But out of curiosity, I try the knob before flipping open my kit.

Unlocked.

When I step inside, I'm surprised to find that it's spotless. So immaculate that it doesn't even look like people actually live here. Picture frames are perfectly hung, couch pillows are so well-placed that they look staged, and it smells so clean.

Too fucking clean.

Antiseptic.

Bleach.

The strong scent of cleaning agents is centered in the foyer, and it dissipates quickly as I move further into the house. Someone cleaned here recently, but only the foyer.

My eyes meticulously linger over every surface, looking for even the smallest signs of a struggle. But there's nothing. Absolutely fucking nothing.

It just doesn't make sense.

There's only one reason you clean one spot with that much bleach.

Blood.

How much blood did Samuel Millington lose the other day?

But why lie about a mugging?

What happened here that they needed to lie?

Realizing I'm not going to find anything in this hallway without luminol, which I'd need to lift from the precinct, I decide to see what I can find in the rest of the house.

Reaching the office, I rummage through some papers on the desk. Only one catches my eye: A printout of the confirmation for a private charter from Greensboro to Wichita three days ago.

What the fuck is in Kansas?

Taking a quick photo with my phone, I tuck it back where I found it before looking over the rest of the main floor.

Room after room and there's nothing but perfectly placed furniture and zero signs of distress. Making my way upstairs, things are even more perfect. A master bedroom the size of my home, filled with diligently folded and hung clothes for both Mr. Millington and Ms. Durant.

No signs of an ID or cell phone having been left behind. Yet, she's disappeared off the face of the Earth. No one has seen or heard from her in the days Mr. Millington has been in the hospital.

Who doesn't race to see their loved one when they nearly die?

Everything is so seemingly fucking perfect, but none of this adds up.

Something happened here.

SAMUEL

"Sitting here doing nothing is driving me fucking insane," I complain as I fidget uncomfortably in this god-forsaken bed. Considering people lay in these beds to fucking die, you'd think they'd be just a bit less unbearable.

Edmund enters the room with three coffees, immediately glancing from me to Grant. Taking note of Grant's face, he asks with a smirk, "Is the kid still complaining?"

"He's fucking incessant." Grant feigns an eye roll. "Can't stand. Has no idea how to do anything on this computer. But he absolutely has to get up to help."

"I left the charter info on the kid's desk early this morning." Handing me a coffee, Edmund questions, "Why Wichita? And what did I miss?"

"It's where Cora's parents are," I respond at nearly the same time as Grant.

"Not much. I was hacking into the backdoor of the local PD." Grant continues to type away on his keyboard. "Did you grab his phone from Abigail?"

"Yeah." Edmund pulls my—no longer blood-covered—phone from his pocket and hands it to Grant.

"So, this Madame," Grant asks as he scrolls through the contacts, "She's how you got in contact with Cora?"

"Yes," I answer. "I mean, it's how I hired her."

I can read the look on Edmund's face without even turning to face him. He was beyond clear that all of my requests should go through Liz.

"At first, anyway," I continue. "But that was weeks ago. And then she stayed."

"Willingly?" Edmund chimes in in jest, a slight poke at Grant.

"Yes, you fucking asshole," I quip.

"And this is the only contact you have for her?" Grant continues, garnering information from me.

"She has an escort website," I answer, "but this is her personal cell."

"Not a burner?"

"No." I shake my head. "I don't think so. She was always annoyed when I reached out to her this way."

"You got him?" Grant looks at Edmund. "I'm going to head home. Take a shower and dig into this; see if I can find out who Madame is. I'll message you if I get anywhere."

"I don't need a fucking babysitter." I look between Edmund and Grant.

"We disagree." Edmund flashes a cheeky smile.

"For fuck's sake." I huff.

"I just want to get out of this bed so that I can feel the least bit helpful in all of this." My voice hitches as I choke on my words, "I just want to fucking find her."

Grant leaves, and Edmund takes a seat. Leaning back in the chair, he stretches out, crossing his feet against the edge of my bed like they're his desk.

"Comfortable?"

"Quite." He smirks. "You?"

"Funny."

"So, Cora." He raises an inquisitive eyebrow. "At what point are you going to fill me in on what's been going on for the past couple of weeks?"

"So, Harper." I turn toward him with a smug look on my face. "I know what she's doing for all of us, but what exactly is she doing for you, Edmund?"

Crossing his arms over his chest, he drops his feet to the floor and stands up. "I'm going to go find that doc. See what I can do about getting you out of bed."

"Really?" I laugh, grabbing my side when it pulls at the stitches. "That serious, huh?"

Completely ignoring me, he leaves the room. Through the window, I can see him flirting shamelessly with one of the young, pretty nurses.

I should be heading home shortly.

***

Apparently, when you nearly die, the doctors are quite insistent on running a barrage of tests before agreeing to let you leave the hospital.

It's been hours of watching my vitals, poking and prodding, changing bandages, and ensuring I would have someone to help me get around for a few days.

It's been fucking hours.

As of thirty minutes ago, they are putting together my discharge paperwork and finding me something to wear home beyond the sexy paper-thin cotton gown I've been wearing.

GRANT
I have a lead.

Cora?

M.

It's a soft lead, but it's a start.

I'll be back at the hospital in about twenty minutes.

We'll come to you.

Funny, Kid.

Seriously.

They're bringing my discharge paperwork now.

CORA

Over the past couple of days, I've managed to stay pretty much confined to my room. An occasional short stint to the kitchen for a granola bar or two to tide me over, then back in my room, safely behind my locked door.

I can't hide from Adam forever, but every day that I do is better than nothing. While the cuts and bruises on my face will heal—and hopefully well—what he did to my back has ruined me. I will never be as valuable as I once was to Madame.

High-end escorts are a fantasy. While fantasies come in many sizes, shapes, and colors, no one is seeking out a mutilated, petite blonde.

I know what that means for me.

My days in this house are limited. She'll keep me around for a while, but when she realizes that I'm not doing anything for her—*that I'm useless*—she'll offload me.

Why didn't she just sell me to Samuel?

A gentle knock on the door startles me from my thoughts. The voice that follows causes bile to rise in my throat.

"Are you going to open the door for me today, little bitch?"

"Not a fucking chance," I shout.

"Why not?" Adam teases as he jiggles the handle. "We had so much fun last time I got to play with you."

We have very different ideas of fun.

Mine definitely doesn't involve being pinned to a counter and having a knife carved through my skin. Or being forced to clean the formerly pristine white granite as sticky blood continued to trickle down my arm. And it absolutely doesn't include any of what he has in mind from the other side of that door.

"It's too bad you don't want to play." My stomach drops when I hear a key slide into the door and the knob turns. Opening the door and stepping inside, a devilish smile spreads across his face as he says, "Because I fucking do."

Trapped, with nowhere to run, I do the only thing I can. Scream.

Adam barrels toward me, covering my mouth with his massive, meaty hand as he drives me into the wall. The open wound on my back grinds against the textured wallpaper, and I scream against his palm in pain.

"What's the matter?" He licks the tear rolling down my face. "I've heard all about your last job. I'd think you like it fucking rough."

"Fuck you!" I yell the muffled words into his palm.

"Fuck me?" he snickers as he throws me across the room. Hitting the bed, I'm unable to keep my balance, and I fall against the mattress. Before I can manage to get up, he's on me.

Even with his forearm wedged firmly between my shoulders, shoving my face into the mattress, and his hips pinning mine to the edge of the bed, I can't miss the distinct sound of him flipping open his switchblade.

The sharp blade in his hand slices effortlessly through my cotton shirt and athletic shorts, leaving me nearly bare beneath him. My screams are muffled by the thick blanket beneath my face, and I continue to fight against the hefty weight pinning me to the bed.

"Feisty little bitch, aren't you?" he laughs over the unmistakable sound of his zipper. I try to fight harder, but he's so fucking heavy, bearing down on me that I can barely move.

"Time to pay up." He shoves a knee between my tightly clenched thighs, his broad leg forcing them to part as he leans his weight against me. Placing vile, rough kisses against his carving on my shoulder, the tip of his cock brushes against my upper thigh.

BANG!

The second the deafening sound echoes through the room, every ounce of his weight is off me.

"What the fuck?" he snarls from behind me.

"I believe I was quite fucking clear that you don't put your cock in her." Lifting my head, I find Madame standing in the doorway, pointing her gun at Adam.

"She's a useless fucking whor—"

BANG!

The bullet punctures the wall a few inches from his head, and he stands motionless as she crosses the room to him. Without another word, she slaps him across the face.

"Do I need to get one of my other men to carve my name into your cock?" She slaps him again. "So every time you want to get your jollies in some tight, young cunt, you remember that my pussies are off-limits?"

"No, ma'am." He vehemently shakes his head.

"Then put your fucking cock away, and get the fuck out of my sight."

Adam zips up so fast that it's a miracle it doesn't guillotine his own dick as he scurries from the room.

"Thank you," I sigh as I pull the blankets around me to cover myself.

"I didn't do it for you." Her tone is flat and cold. "If I let him fuck your worthless cunt, it's just letting the others know they can get away with fucking my girls for free. My clientele isn't looking for sloppy seconds in working-class spunk."

It doesn't matter.

I don't care why she did it.

"Clean yourself up," she demands as she walks toward the door. "You're bleeding all over my Egyptian cotton sheets."

SAMUEL

"Samuel!" Abigail's name carries through the house. "He's got something."

For someone who I'm pretty sure absolutely despised me a few weeks ago, Grant has been working tirelessly to help find Cora. Everyone has.

And I'm really not certain why.

Steadily making my way across the house, I find Grant exactly where I left him a few hours ago. Hunched over a laptop at my dining room table, clicking away at the keyboard.

The phone number I gave him didn't get us very far. He managed to trace it to a business in Greensboro. *The Emerald Gentlemen's Club.* William paid a visit that night, only to find that the address was nothing more than an abandoned lot.

It's taken a substantial amount of digging to wade through the shell corporations, but we finally found Madame. Or at least her name. *Anneliese Rotschilde.*

Likely not her real name, but the same name each and every one of her properties and businesses are listed under. Right down to the monthly bill of her internet provider.

We found her two hours ago, and as much as I was raring to go in guns blazing, the others were happy to allow Grant a little more time to do what it is that he does best —or at least what it has made him a large fortune.

"I told you," he says, spinning the laptop in my direction as I enter the room. "You don't become as powerful and invisible as she is without some help. And a little dirt on some important people in powerful places."

"Fuck." The word escapes me as I stare at the screen before me. "Do I even want to know what you have buried somewhere?"

Grant laughs with a haughtiness, letting me know that he's got dirt well beyond the devils.

"Now what?" I question as Grant slides a burner phone across the table to Edmund.

> I'm looking for some entertainment.

MADAME
You must have the wrong number.

> It's the right number.

I'm certain.

An acquaintance gave it to me a few
months back.

What friend?

Samuel Millington.

And your name?

Edmund.

???

"Your whole name," I say over his shoulder as he reads
her message. "She's going to vet you. Make sure you can
afford her."

Parker.

He had informed me that for the right
price, I could get whatever I wanted.

Show me you're serious.

0384930103434. 403943274039274392.

"How much?" Edmund queries as he looks at the off-
shore routing numbers.

"One hundred thousand is her buy-in."

"Are you fucking serious?" Edmund spins in his seat.
"And that doesn't even get me pussy?"

Pulling out his own phone, Edmund sighs as he makes the transfer. "You fucking owe me."

And what is it that you want Mr. Parker?

Is it possible to see what you have to offer?

403927 Glendale Ln, Greensboro

2 hours.

Do not be late.

EDMUND

"Are you sure this is the right place?" Samuel questions from the concealment of the backseat as we pull to a stop before an office building.

Pulling out my phone, I send a text.

Here.

MADAME
22nd floor.

"Wish me luck," I grab my things from the passenger seat. Dialing Samuel's number, I slip my phone into the breast pocket of my jacket.

As much as he's dying to, Samuel can't come inside. Madame, her men, and several of her women know his face. But he's adamant that he knows what is happening while I am inside.

Walking into the building, I mumble to Samuel, "And if I end up fucking dead, kid…"

I pass reception, head to the elevator bank and press the call button. It comes promptly, and I push the button for the twenty-second floor.

"Mr. Parker," a slightly older, yet very attractive, woman greets me when the elevator doors ding open. "I have a few ladies for you to meet."

"Perfect," I respond as we make our way down the hall. "I'm looking for a woman that can handle my… um…interests."

"And those would be?"

"Pain."

Not having to lie makes this really fucking easy.

"Giving or receiving?" she asks.

"**Definitely** giving," I emphasize as she pushes open the door to our left.

"The ladies." She gestures to the wall of gorgeous women dressed in designer lingerie.

"Hmmm," I say as I walk around the room.

Fuck, I would eagerly take most of them home.

At least one of them would make a good little pain slut for me.

"They are all quite magnificent," I turn back to Madame, "but my acquaintance had a blonde that, from his account of their interactions, I can only imagine would be exactly what I'm looking for."

"I'm sorry," she draws out her faux apology, "but Cora isn't available right now."

"Cora, yes." I play ignorant. "That was her name. What would it cost for her to be available?"

"I'm sorry, Mr. Parker. She's going to be unavailable for at least a week or two. I'm sure one of these other girls would more than meet your needs."

"Maybe this will cover it?" I pull a matte-black USB drive from my pocket.

"And what is that?"

"Senator Harrison. Governor Kendrick. Congressman Covington." I place it on the table before me. "Need I go on? The men and women on here might be very interested to know that the woman they trust with their entertainment is building quite a collection of blackmail."

She swipes the drive from the table and lets out a rattled heavy breath.

"Powerful fucking men and women who would more than happily wipe you from existence to protect themselves," I continue. "And before you start getting any grandiose ideas, I have some fucking powerful friends in very influential places who have copies."

"What do you want?" she curtly asks.

"Cora."

"Fine." She picks up the phone on the desk and huffs, "Get Cora dressed and bring her down here."

She places the receiver back on the cradle, and I continue as I wait for them to bring Cora to me, "You and anyone that works for you will stay far the fuck away from Adelaide Cove."

She nods in agreement.

"Samuel Millington," her eyes go wide with surprise when I speak his name, "Cora, and me. Understood?"

CORA

"Open up," Adam's voice bellows from the other side of the door as he jiggles the knob.

"Not a fucking chance," I snarl.

He hits it hard, and the whole door rattles as I faintly hear the sound of wood splintering. Slamming against it again, it gives way, and he comes hurdling into the room.

"Don't fucking touch me," I grit through my teeth as I scramble across the bed to get away from him.

"I'll do whatever the fuck I want." He grabs my ankle and roughly yanks me across the bed to him as I flail and kick my feet. The heel of my foot makes contact with his jaw, and he grunts as it whips his head to the side.

"You fucking little bitch," he snarls as he roughly grabs at my shirt and pulls me upright. Bending down, he throws me over his shoulder and carries me from the room.

My fists pound against his back, and I yell, "Fucking put me down," as he carries me down the hall toward the elevator. Swiping his access card, he carries me into the elevator and drops me on the floor.

"Is that what you wanted?" he snickers as I groan from the pain of the impact. "Now, get the fuck up."

When I don't do as he demands, he fists my hair and pulls me from the floor as I try to help bring myself to my feet. "Fuck! I'm getting up."

Not releasing his tight hold on my hair, my scalp burns as he uses his hold to force me from the elevator. Terrified of where we're going, my steps are small and staggered as he continues to force me down the long corridor.

"She'll fucking kill you if you fuck me, and you fucking know it."

A dark laugh bursts from him as we reach a door at the end of the hall.

"Oh, this is going to be so much worse for you." His next words petrify me to the core as he begins to push open the door. "She just sold you."

Adam shoves me through the door, and I fall into the chest of a dark-haired, middle-aged man with a beard.

Gripping my upper arms, he helps to steady me before returning his attention to Madame. "We good here?"

"Yes," she exhales. "Just get her the fuck out of here."

"I look forward to never seeing you again." His tone is cordial, but a snarky smirk ticks at the corner of his mouth. Placing his hand on the small of my back, he leads me from the room to the elevator.

He ushers me into the empty cab, pushes the button for the lobby, and says, "I have her. We're on our way down."

My brows furrow in confusion, not understanding who he's talking to.

"Are you okay?" He turns his gaze to me, delicately tilting my face as his eyes roam over the marble of bruises on my face.

Nodding my head, I fight back the tears at the first bit of gentleness I've been shown in almost a week, and mutter, "Yes."

The elevator dings, and he places his hand against the small of my back again as the elevator doors begin to open.

Opening to the lobby, my heart stops, and I can't breathe.

Am I dreaming?

"Samuel!" I scream his name through the tears streaming down my face as I run through the lobby to reach him. Crashing into him, a pained grunt rattles him, and he struggles to stay on his feet.

"Careful," Samuel winces.

"How?" My hands roam his chest and touch his face, trying to convince myself that he's real. "I...I watched... you die."

"I told you, love." He cups my face. "I wasn't letting you go. Satan himself couldn't pull me from you."

"This is real fucking sweet and all," the dark-haired man interrupts the two of us, "but can you two do this anywhere else?"

SAMUEL

Three days later

It's funny how a near-death experience really puts things into perspective.

And not just for the person who almost died.

After thinking I had died, and mourning me for days, only to find me alive, Cora has realized that she cares about me too much to willingly walk away from me.

Not that I would've let her.

The things I did before meeting her, the urges I still fight, aren't going anywhere. They won't ever go away, but she's open to finding a way to help me manage them.

I can be good for her.

EDMUND
I'll be there in 3 minutes.

Ok.

Will picked the gift up.

He's going to meet us there.

Perfect.

I want to be good for her.

But I need to do this first.

Trying to be quiet and not disturb Cora, I slip from the bed. I grab a pair of sweatpants and a T-shirt from the bench at the foot of the bed and slip them on in the dark and head downstairs. By the time I reach the front door, Edmund is pulling to a stop out front.

Sneaking out the front door, I slip into Edmund's car, and we make our way down the drive and toward The Preserves. A whole development of mini-mansions burying all of our dirty little secrets.

He makes a right-hand turn, and we head through a construction gate to a section of the community still under development. William's G-Class is parked at the makeshift curb, and Edmund pulls in behind him. As he parks, Will opens the trunk to reveal my gift.

Well, my gift to Cora.

Adam Rodgers.

Judging by the looks of his face, Will has already spent a great deal of time with him. For the massive enforcer that he is, he's crying like a bitch as Will pulls him from the back of the SUV and shoves him toward the empty construction site.

I follow behind them, my gait is still a little slow from the pain in my side, so they reach the framing for the pending foundation before I do.

Catching up to them, I slide the blindfold from Adam's face and thoroughly enjoy watching his eyes widen as he takes in the ghost standing before him.

"I see you remember me." I can't help the smile that spreads across my face. "Do you also remember what I told you the last time I saw you?"

He shakes his head as I hold out my hand to Will. Flipping open the blade he pulled from Adam's pocket earlier, he places it in my palm.

"I told you," I plunge the blade into his gut, "I would fucking kill you for touching her."

Pulling out the blade, I sink it through his flesh again and again. His stomach. Chest. Neck. Thigh. Over and over. Not stopping until I can barely lift my arm. His dead, lifeless body only standing because William and Edmund are holding him up for me.

My hand is covered in his blood, and crimson splatters of him cover my arm and formerly white undershirt.

Closing the ruby-red knife, I place it in my pocket as Will and Edmund drop Adam into the abyss behind him.

"I'll fill it in." William nods at us. "Get him back home before Cora realizes he's gone."

The ride back to my place in Edmund's car is silent, not a word spoken between us. Words aren't needed.

I would do the same for him.

Grant.

Liz.

No questions asked if someone dared take something that belonged to one of them.

Sneaking back into the house with the same stealthiness I used to leave, I'm hoping to get showered and back in bed without waking Cora. I'll deal with disposing of any evidence in the morning.

"Where did you go?" Her voice is soft and concerned as I step through the threshold to our room.

A bright light and her terrified gasp fill the room when she flips on her bedside table.

CHAPTER
FORTY-EIGHT

CORA

"Sam—" My voice trembles at the sight of him. His hands are red. It stains his shirt where it must have splattered across him and where he tried to wipe his hands clean. His face is freckled with droplets of dried blood.

It's fucking everywhere.

"Wh...where did you go?" I ask, even though I'm terrified of the answer.

"It's not what you think, love." I shake my head as he pulls the bloody shirt from his body. "I did this for you."

"For me?" My voice rises as he walks toward the bathroom as though he just returned from a late-night jog. "What the fuck did you do?"

Reaching into his pocket as he walks, he tosses some-thing onto the bed and disappears into the bathroom. He turns on the water as I hesitate to reach for whatever is at the end of the bed.

Taking a deep breath, I reach down and wrap my hands around the cool metal. The moment I touch it, I know it is.

Adam's switchblade.

It's covered in dried blood. The same blood that Samuel is stained crimson with.

He killed him.

Sliding from the bed, I head into the bathroom and slip into the shower behind him. Wrapping my arms around him, I place my forehead against his back. "I'm sorry... I just.... I just thought..."

"I've told you, love." He turns to face me, and his hands slide along my jaw as he tips my face up to his. "You're all I need."

His lips crash into mine as he pulls my face into his. Parting my lips, his tongue darts between them and sweeps over mine, and he drags me under the stream of water with him. The droplets rain over us as he kisses me until I am beyond breathless.

The sins of the night trickle down our bodies, scarlet water swirling at our feet as he grips my thighs and drives me into the cool marble wall of the shower.

With one hand on my ass, he uses the other to align himself with my entrance. Driving into me with such force that I yelp, and he laces his fingers around my throat.

"You." He slams into me and tightens his grip around my neck, repeating his motions with each subsequent word. "You. Are. It. For. Me."

As I struggle to breathe, he continues to thrust with brutal force. "All. I. Fucking. Want."

My nails claw at his back, and my thighs squeeze around his waist as he fucks me with animalistic need. Wave after wave of electricity surges through my body as he brings me over the edge.

"Sam," I cry out as he thrusts in deep, but it's a mere whisper through the vise around my neck.

Releasing my throat, he turns off the water. Still buried inside of me, he kisses across my breasts and up my neck before whispering, "I'm not fucking done with you yet, love."

His strong arms wrap firmly around me, and he plunders my mouth as he carries me to the bed. Laying me down gently, he slides in and out of me in slow, steady strokes before pulling himself from me.

Gripping my hands, he spins me on the bed until my head is hanging over the edge. He rubs the head of his cock against my lips and commands, "Open wide for me, love."

He taps the soft skin of the tip teasingly against my lips, and I dart out my tongue.

"Is this what you want?" He presses between my lips, and my tastebuds are flooded with the slight tang of my arousal as he slides over my tongue. "Show me how much you enjoy sucking the sweetness of your delicious cunt off my cock."

His hips thrust lightly, pushing his length repeatedly over my tongue as I hollow my cheeks and diligently suck every bit of my flavor from him.

Gripping beneath my chin, he tips my head further off the bed, allowing him to push into my throat with ease. He slides every inch down before stilling.

"Give me your hands," he commands as he pulls far enough from me that I can suck in a breath. Sliding back down my throat, he pulls my left hand behind his back. Leaning forward, and pushing in even deeper, he presses my other hand between my thighs and slides my fingers over my clit. "I want to watch you as I fuck your throat."

He begins slow, languid strokes over my tongue and down my throat, his eyes fixated on the fingers rubbing between my thighs. Rubbing over and around my already sensitive clit, I groan around him. In response, Samuel changes his pace. His strokes become faster and deeper.

My fingers rub diligently over my clit while he fucks my face, needing desperately to come.

"That's it," he encourages me, "show me how much you love it when I fucking use you. How much you love being my little fuck toy."

Adding his fingers to mine, we rub fervently at my clit as he rapidly fucks my throat. Blackness creeps over the edges of my vision as he deprives me of air and works me toward the edge.

My body explodes so hard that every muscle in my body convulses, and I scream around the cock buried in my throat.

"FUCK!" Samuel roars as he comes down my throat. Sliding himself from my mouth, he climbs onto the bed and pulls me to his chest. Holding me against him, he brushes the hair from my face as I slowly catch my breath.

"All I want, love." He softly kisses my forehead. "Forever."

CHAPTER
FORTY-NINE

DETECTIVE MICHALES

Walking into Latte Da, the last person I expected to see this soon was Samuel Millington. Just a few days out of the hospital, fresh off the back of the disappearance of his so-called girlfriend, he's standing at the counter like it's any other Tuesday.

Clearing my throat as I approach him, I nod my head as he turns to face me. "Mr. Millington."

"Detective Michales." He feigns a smile before turning back toward the baristas hastily making coffees.

"I know you've been to the precinct to discuss the details of your alleged mugging—"

"Alleged?" He quickly turns to face me with a scoff. "I had twenty-two stitches, ruptured my spleen, and nearly died. I think we can move past the alleged disposition."

"Samuel?" the barista calls from behind the counter as she places two coffees down.

He promptly places a sizable tip in the jar on the counter and grabs the two cups before him. Turning back to face me, he quips, "Always a pleasure, Detective."

Without another word, he walks to the door and uses his shoulder to nudge it open.

Turning on my heel and following behind him, I match his brisk pace as he makes his way down the sidewalk. "I've actually been wanting to speak with you regarding Cora Durant. It appears that she disappeared the same day you wound up in the hospital."

"She's missing?" He places one of the cups on the roof of his car with a furrowed brow.

"Yes." My voice becomes more authoritative as he opens the driver's side door. "Missing."

"Cora. Love." He dips his head into the car and extends one of the coffees to a passenger. "Detective Michales seems to think that you went missing earlier this week."

She leans over the console toward the open door, and I repeatedly blink my eyes as though they are deceiving me.

"Missing?" Her tone is inquisitive. "Why on earth would you think that?"

I stare at her silently, still in disbelief that she's sitting before me.

Even more so that she's still alive.

"Samuel graciously flew me out to visit my nana for a few days." She looks at him adoringly. "Isn't that sweet of him?"

"Yes." My eyes suspiciously roam over Mr. Millington as he gingerly slides into the seat beneath him. "Very."

I don't believe a fucking word of it.

Every word from their mouths reeks of bullshit.

Samuel.

Edmund.

Grant.

And now, even Cora.

"If you don't need any more proof that she's still alive," Mr. Millington begins pulling his door shut. "We have somewhere to be."

Shaking my head, he shuts the door, and I watch the two of them pull away. They might as well be riding off into the sunset because every fucking lie they've just spewed will have some magical thread of evidence to back it up.

Because they always do.

Sooner or later, I'll find something.

Something is bound to rattle them.

SAMUEL

Nearly One Month Later

Pulling into the valet and slamming on the brakes, my tires screech to a stop. I glance at the time on the dash, and I push the car door open.

Fuck.

I'm so fucking late.

Walking at a swift pace, I make my way up the walkway and to the doors of the tasting room. As I push it open, I immediately spot Cora sitting alone at the bar.

She's fucking impossible to miss.

Sitting with her back to me, I take a moment to enjoy her as I slowly walk toward the bar. Her luxurious blonde hair is twisted and braided into a tousled bun, fully exposing her long, slender neck. The little black dress she chose for this evening has thin straps running over her shoulders, leaving every inch of her spine bare. The satin skims over the shoulder marred by Madame. The 'M' savagely carved into her back is now covered with a tattoo of an ornate 'S' flanked by flowers—branding her as mine.

So much of her on display, yet she pulls it off with sophistication and grace as she savors the glass of Cabernet in her hand.

She was fucking made for this world.

The one that I give her.

Stepping behind her, I bend down and place a kiss on the crook of her neck. Stealing a quick nip before I stand, I whisper, "You look fucking gorgeous, love."

"And you're late," she quips with a smirk.

Taking the seat beside her, I order a glass of Shiraz for myself before asking, "What will it take to make it up to you?"

"I don't think you can afford it." Her tone is serious as she teases me.

"Try me."

"Two grand." She raises a mischievous eyebrow.

"Done," I counter. "Do you take credit?"

She runs her hands down her sides, over the dress that is hugging every curve of her body. "Do I look like I take card?"

Reaching to the breast pocket of my jacket, I pull out my wallet and retrieve twenty hundred dollar bills. Discreetly sliding them over the bar toward her purse, she scoops them up and tucks them inside.

"Forgiven." She shoots me a smug smile.

The vineyard has become somewhat of a second home to us. We visit a couple of times a week for dinner, a late-night stroll through the vines, and occasionally, a quick, dirty fuck in the wine cellar.

Tonight's dinner is special, though. It's been a tad over a month since I nearly saw what life looked like on the other side of Hell's gates. And exactly one month since Edmund helped me bring Cora back home.

"What kept you, anyway?" she asks as she takes a sip of her wine.

"I was picking up something for you." I reach into my jacket pocket, and she grabs my wrist to stop me.

"We've talked about this." Her voice is soft and tender.

"I don't need a ring on your finger or a piece of paper filed with the state to know that you're mine." I pull the envelope from my pocket and slide it across the bar. "Now, shut up and let me fucking spoil you."

Lifting the envelope from the bar, she carefully pulls the paperwork out of it and begins reading over the contents.

"You didn't!" she gasps, tossing the papers onto the counter and throwing herself into my arms. Her body melts into mine, and I press my lips against hers. Her tongue darts between her teeth and flicks against my lips, and I lightly groan with need. Pulling back, she looks up at me, "How did you--"

"Know you wanted it?" I pull her tightly to me. "You can't get enough of this place. It only made sense that we could come here whenever you wanted."

"Sam—"

"Shhh." I press my finger to her lips. "Do I need to remind you that I take care of what's mine? And I'd buy you the fucking moon if you told me you wanted it, love."

Gripping her chin, I place a rough kiss against her lips before speaking against them. "Anything. Everything. Forever."

I slip behind the bar and grab a bottle from the fridge. Gliding my hand into hers and lacing our fingers together, I pull her from the bar. "If you're done complaining about this lavish gift that I've given you, I'd like to take you on a tour of your new vineyard."

Squeezing my hand, she struggles to keep up as I lead her through the tasting room to the veranda overlooking the entire property.

"I think you'll be quite interested to learn how they age and bottle that Cabernet you enjoy so much." I continue to walk her around the corner and toward the wine cellar below the tasting room. "Or their sparkling wine. It's absolutely titillating."

CORA

"You know I'm not big on sparkling wine," I correct him as we take the steps down to the cellar. He leads me through the dimly lit corridors of barrels in silence until we're tucked away in a dark corner.

"You might just be surprised how much you enjoy it." He uncorks the bottle in his hands, and I squeak, startled by the pop and the cold spray across my chest. Icy droplets drip down my chest and beneath the plunging cowl neckline of my dress.

Leaning forward, he places wet kisses over my chest, licking the splattered sparkling Chardonnay from me. The bottle still in his hand, he slips his fingers beneath the thin spaghetti strap of my dress and slides them from my shoulders. They skim down my arms, and the top of my dress pools around my waist as he continues to lick and suck the sweet droplets from my skin.

My chest rises and falls as whimpers tremble from my lips. Samuel's tongue swirls around my nipple with finesse. Lifting the bottle, he pours the bubbles over my breast, and I bite my lip and groan as the frigid stream trickles down my skin to the awaiting warmth of his mouth.

Leaving a quick stinging bite, he kneels on the floor between my feet. Liquid drips from his chin, and he stares up at me with an insatiable hunger in his eyes. He pulls my dress and panties over my hips and down my legs, leaving me leaning against the cold, concrete wall in nothing but my heels.

Lifting the bottle to his lips, he tips it back with a devilish smirk. He pulls it from his mouth, hoists my leg over his shoulder, and plunges his face between my thighs. The frosty bubbles in his mouth tickle against my pussy as he licks voraciously at my clit.

"Oh my go—" I grip his head and grind against his mouth, needing more of him. Knowing exactly what I need, he teases around my entrance with his finger, and I groan, "Please..."

He continues to rub against me, but it's hard and foreign. Opening my eyes, I find him teasing me with the rim of the wine bottle.

"Sam—" I begin to protest, but he slides the neck of the smooth, cold glass into me, and I melt over it with a moan. Thrusting the bottle into me, he continues to feast on me with a feral need until I'm writhing over his face and coming around the bottle. The rush of pleasure shoots through me, and my legs tremble so hard I struggle to stay upright.

Leisurely pulling the bottle from me, Samuel places a soft kiss against my clit and lowers my leg before standing. He takes a drink from the bottle and moans as he swallows it.

"Open wide." He grips my chin, squeezing with enough pressure to force my mouth open as he tips my head back. He lifts the bottle to his lips instead of mine. Tossing the bottle to the floor, he leans over me and spills the contents of his mouth into mine. Pressing my lips shut, his voice is gravelly when he commands, "Swallow like a good little whore."

He waits for me to swallow, watching me obey him with pride while he undoes his pants. They slide down his thighs, exposing his thick, throbbing cock. Gripping the back of my thighs and lifting me around his waist, he claims my mouth as he slams into me.

My hands fist the lapels of his jacket as he drives hard and deep. His eyes lock onto mine, and he quickly has me screaming and moaning with every powerful thrust into me. Squeezing my legs around his waist, my thighs shake relentlessly as the building release in my core travels through every synapse in my body with a rush as I scream his name.

"Fuck, love," he groans, burying himself in me, "I fucking love it when you scream for me."

Gripping my ass, he pulls me from the wall.   He continues his claim on my mouth, and he lays me on the cold, stone floor. Settling between my knees, he plunges back into me. He reaches over my body and wraps both hands around my throat. He fucks me hard and fast, his knees digging into the stone beneath us as he leans on my throat. My mouth falls open, both from needing to scream and gasping unsuccessfully for air.

"Are you going to cry for me too, love?" he grunts as he tightens his grip and increases his already relentless, brutal pace.

Tears well in my eyes, unable to handle the burning pain in my deprived lungs. Hovering on the verge of death, my pussy clenches around him as my back arches from the cold, rough ground. A painfully blissful wave crashes through me, and the tears fall from my eyes as I come again.

"So. Fucking. Beautiful," Samuel grunts through three rough, deep thrusts before burying to the hilt with a groan. His cock twitches inside of me, and he releases my throat as he spills inside of me.

Resting over my body, he tenderly wipes the tears from my face as he kisses over my cheeks.

"So fucking perfect, Cora." His lips dust over mine, and I can feel him smiling against me. "You're fucking it for me, love."

Staring up at him, I whisper, "Forever."

EPILOGUE

SAMUEL

A Few Days Later

Sneaking out of the house for the third morning in a row, I drive to the park a few miles away. It's a popular spot in town for early-morning runners. Most days it's crowded, and the nearby lot is packed full of cars. But not this morning. There are only a handful of cars in the lot.

The temperature dropped unseasonably cold overnight. The cool air and the light drizzle falling from the sky were apparently enough to keep most of the regulars at home.

But not her.

The petite blonde runs along the edge of the park. It's too cold for the tiny spandex running shorts and sports bra she is wearing, yet perfect for causing her hardened nipples to jut against the pink fabric. Her tits bounce in rhythm with the sway of her ponytail with every stride she takes.

The reason I'm here.

Stepping from the warmth of the car into the cool morning air, the light rain dampens my hair as I walk toward the running trail. I follow it between the trees, continuing a little deeper into the woods before leaving the trail and waiting out of sight.

For her.

It isn't long before I can hear the pad of her shoes on the wet path. My heart pounds, and my cock throbs in anticipation. She jogs toward me, unaware I'm hiding in the brush. Oblivious that I'm coming for her.

Barreling at her as she jogs past, I scoop her into my arms and carry her off the trail with ease. Arms and legs flailing, she screams as I force her to the ground. She sinks into the sodden grass as I smother her with my body.

I fucking need her.

Tearing at my belt, I can't get it off fast enough. I wrap it around her neck and pull it tight before ripping her tight little shorts over her perfectly round ass. Shoving her thighs apart with my knee, she twists and thrashes beneath me as I press inside of her.

"That's it. Fucking fight me," I groan. "It makes your screams that much fucking sweeter when you come for me."

Fuck, I've missed this.

With my hand between her shoulders, I press her into the ground as I tug at the leather around her throat. It muffles her screams, keeping them just for me as I drive my hips against her ass.

It's too fucking good.

"You will fucking come for me," I growl. Sucking my thumb into my mouth, I cover it in saliva and press it to her ass. I rub around the hole. "One way or another. You will fucking come for me."

Plunging my thumb into her, I work it into her tight hole with the same rapid, deep thrusts of my cock. She can fight me, but she can't fight her body. Her perfect cunt clenches around my cock as her ass squeezes around my thumb, and her body quivers beneath me as she comes undone for me.

"Fuck!" I drive into her with a roar as I fill her cunt with my cum. Slipping my thumb out of her, I can't help but slap her round ass as I slide my cock from her hole.

"And good morning to you too," Cora pants as she breathlessly rolls onto her back and shimmies her wet shorts back over her hips.

Helping her to her feet, she stretches onto her toes and presses her lips to mine. Pulling back, she mutters with a chuckle, "You're a sick fuck."

Wrapping my arm over her shoulder and pulling her into my body as I walk back toward the cars, I kiss the top of her head. "And you're equally as depraved, love. It's why you're so fucking perfect for me."

"Forever," she replies as we reach her car. "See you at home?"

"I'll be right behind you." I shut her door and head across the lot to mine. Settling into the driver's seat, I lift my cell phone from the cup holder to find seven missed calls from all of the devils and a voicemail from Edmund.

I press play. His voice, from what I can understand between the muffled static of the signal cutting in and out, sounds frantic. "Harper...too far...fucking dead."

THANK YOU FOR READING

I hope you enjoyed the beginning of the Samuel and Cora's story!

If you did, the best support you can give to an indie author, like myself, is to tell others about my book. Reviews left on Goodreads, Amazon, or anywhere else you are comfortable truly mean the world to me.

Want to know what happens next in Adelaide Cove? Check out the series!

ALSO BY J.L. QUICK

THE SAVAGELY DEPRAVED SERIES

- Dark Devils
- Family Ties
- Brutal Bond (Coming July 2024)
- Vicious Deceit (Coming September 2024)

THE MEN OF CLUB TRISKELION SERIES

- Owned (Coming August 2024)
- Bound (Coming October 2024)
- Primal (Coming November 2024)

THE BOTTICELLI BROTHERHOOD SERIES

- Sold to the Syndicate
- Capo Dei Capi's Daughter
- Indebted to the Enemy
- Falling for the Mafia Dom

THE MARCANO MOGULS SERIES

- Tryst
- Crave

- Intern
- Savage